Death by Theory

Death by Theory
A Tale of Mystery and Archaeological Theory

REVISED EDITION

Adrian Praetzellis

ALTAMIRA
PRESS

A division of
ROWMAN & LITTLEFIELD PUBLISHERS, INC.
Lanham • New York • Toronto • Plymouth, UK

Published by AltaMira Press
A division of Rowman & Littlefield Publishers, Inc.
A wholly owned subsidary of The Rowman & Littlefield Publishing Group, Inc.
4501 Forbes Boulevard, Suite 200, Lanham, Maryland 20706
http://www.altamirapress.com

Estover Road, Plymouth PL6 7PY, United Kingdom

British Library Cataloguing in Publication Information Available

Library of Congress Cataloging-in-Publication Data

Praetzellis, Adrian, 1952–
    Death by theory : a tale of mystery and archaeological theory / Adrian Praetzellis.—
Rev. ed.
        p.   cm.
    Includes bibliographical references and index.
    ISBN 978-0-7591-1957-4 (cloth : alk. paper)
    ISBN 978-0-7591-1958-1 (pbk. : alk. paper)
    ISBN 978-0-7591-1959-8 (electronic)
    1. Archaeology.   2. Archaeology—Methodology.   I. Title.
CC72.P73   2011
930.1072—dc22

                                                    2010043857

♾ ™ The paper used in this publication meets the minimum requirements of American National Standard for Information Sciences—Permanence of Paper for Printed Library Materials, ANSI/NISO Z39.48-1992.

Printed in the United States of America

CONTENTS

CONTENTS

PREFACE TO THE SECOND EDITION

No one would have thought that *Death by Theory* would have archaeologists all over the world clamoring for a second edition. And in fact they didn't.

Nevertheless, the first edition did achieve modest success in the unappreciated field of archaeology/mystery/textbooks, which is why today I'm still pounding out profundities on the old MacBook.

Secondhand textbooks are cheaper than new ones since neither author nor publisher gets paid. Authors like me and publishers like mine make a living by selling new books. We both have a clear incentive to create new editions of popular textbooks, and it is legitimate when there's a good educational reason. Looking back on these revisions, I think the second edition of *Death by Theory* is significantly better than the first. Several reviewers of the 2000 edition made good suggestions for improvement (thank you), some of which I've actually followed:

- There's a new chapter on agency and neoevolutionary theory.

- The "Talking Points" and "Further Reading" sections have been expanded, and the references updated.

- Someone recommended that adding illustrations of the action would help develop atmosphere and make the story more fun, so I did it.

- Finally, I'm indebted to the reviewer who wrote that sometimes the language sounded like I had "swallowed a dictionary." He or she was right, and I've tried to fix it.

At least one inquiring mind wanted to know how my character Ian Nigel Tuliver got his name.

First, I wanted two forenames that sounded English—you know, English from England. There are few creatures so arrogant as a snooty English academic, and picturing the obnoxious Tuliver as this type helped me bring him to life. The surname Tuliver is an homage to Michael "Mouse" Tolliver, a creation of novelist Armistead Maupin. Not that the characters are at all alike. I just liked the sound of it.

Adrian Praetzellis
Lucia, California
19 July 2010

ACKNOWLEDGMENTS

This book wouldn't have been possible without Mary, who gave me the freedom to play writer. AltaMira Press founder Mitch Allen was kind enough (or perhaps weird enough) to take a chance on this mystery/theory thing. Since this is the second edition, it seems not to have been a bad business decision. My writing coach Penny Warner laughed at the funny bits and told me not to give up. Not quite two years old, my granddaughter Diana didn't help with this book at all. But perhaps someday she might like to see her name in print and know that I was thinking of her.

The anonymous reviewers—they know who they are, though I don't—of both the first and second editions were kind enough to spend their time looking over the manuscript and making pages of helpful suggestions. Of course, none of these worthy scholars is responsible for errors of fact or interpretation that they may have overlooked; that's all my doing.

"A" IS FOR ARCHAEOLOGY

In Which Dr. Green and Mr. Doyle Are Enlisted

With massive breasts and great globelike ass, the image flickering on the screen was a vision of fecund sensuality. An object of erotic desire, even religious devotion, or so he supposed.

Sean Doyle stifled a yawn and considered whether or not he could discreetly bail on the performance. As a rule, he wasn't immune to feminine charms. It was just that this particular woman was three inches high and several thousand years old. **Neolithic** archaeology had never held much interest for Sean. Too many rocks and no written sources to keep in check what seemed to him to be an overactive archaeological imagination.

In fact, this entire trip to the Society for American Archeology's annual meeting was turning out to be something of a dud. The only morning session he had marked with a check on his conference program—a series of papers on cemetery **archaeology**—had been filled to overflowing by writers of midlist mystery novels whose protagonists were spunky forensic anthropologists with idiosyncratic pets and names like Kate and Kinsey. Sean had been forced to sit outside the hall and think about the $110 registration fee.

The speaker droned on, interrupted by her sneezing fits. More slides of enormously endowed figurines. Sean tapped his companion's shoulder and whispered so close to her ear that his cheek brushed one of her gray curls and he smelled the patchouli.

"Do you want to get outta here?" he hissed. "I can't stand any more of 'The World According to **Marija Gimbutas.**'"

"Not a fan of ecofeminist archaeology, Sean?" she goaded. "OK. I'm starting to snooze myself. But let's be quiet about it. The speaker's a friend of mine."

They got up and shuffled as quietly as they could along the row of chairs to the side aisle.

"I can see its appeal, though," he continued when they were out of the meeting room. "You know—the idea that the Neolithic in southeastern Europe was a peaceful, egalitarian . . ."

". . . matriarchal, goddess-worshipping era. Yes, it appeals to me, too. But, well . . ." His colleague paused with a lopsided half smile.

"Yeah, I know what you're going to say, *Doctor* Green: there's just not much evidence that it ever happened."

Hannah Green noted the cynical edge to her nephew's voice and knew that she had been too free with her own critiques. *That's the problem with hanging out with cynical old archaeologists like me*, she told herself. *Sean's at the point where he doesn't believe anything an archaeologist says that isn't a matter of empirical fact. My fault. Damn it.*

"But it's a nice, optimistic story all the same," she said with a grin, resolving to be less critical in the future. Or at least when he could hear her.

The two sat side by side on the vinyl-covered bench, their backs against the wall, vaguely watching the conference-goers bustle past. They made an unremarkable couple, the young man and his archaeologist aunt. Most who bothered to spare them a glance took the pair as student and professor: Sean Doyle looked younger than his twenty-three years and hardly even resented being carded at bars anymore. Blond-haired—well, not exactly blond, more that mousy brown that turns light in the summer and darkens up by January—he was good-looking in a high school jock sort of a way. He was inclined to be taciturn, a trait derived (or so his aunt believed) from his childhood in the upper Midwest and an Episcopalian father. But the casual observer who guessed "undergrad" got it wrong. With a six-month-old anthropology BA in his pocket, Sean was out in the world and scouting around for whatever might turn up in the way of a career. And graduate school in archaeology seemed like a good enough way to put off the decision for another few years.

"Listen, **boychik**, grad school is a big step," his aunt had declared with much finger wagging at his graduation party. Sean had always been a great romantic, dropping everything for the sake of each new obsession.

2

"Take my advice," said Hannah, "and go find out what archaeology is about before you commit to it. Spend a year with a government agency or, even better, a contract archaeology firm. Learn how archaeology is really done, then decide if it's what you want to do."

It had seemed like good advice. And besides, his mother refused to come up with any money for tuition unless he followed her sister's suggestion. The latter consideration had settled it, and Sean had spent eight of the last twelve months working as a grunt for archaeological consultants between Illinois and Missouri, digging square holes and tramping through blackberry bushes allegedly for the purpose of archaeological survey.

Now it was May. He was out of work and here at the SAA meeting for the sole purpose of scoping out the employment possibilities. His aunt was hardly one of the big shots in North American archaeology, but she should have a few contacts. Or so he hoped. Sean's fantasy was to work his way west and south as an itinerant archaeologist. California would be nice. Dig during the day, then down to the beach for a cool social life. But all he'd been offered was a place on a pipeline survey in Oklahoma.

"It's a nice story?" quizzed Sean. "Is that all archaeology is—just a bunch of stories? Don't archaeologists think of themselves as scientists anymore? Testing theories and that sort of thing?"

Right now, Sean was more concerned with whether or not they had blackberry bushes in Oklahoma, and whether ten dollars an hour for schlepping dirt was likely to go farther there than it did in Illinois.

"And just *how many* units did *you* take in archaeology?"

Hannah regretted her sarcasm as soon as the words were out of her mouth. Her ability to give emphasis to words as if she were saying them in capital letters was a useful trait in a university lecturer, but some people found it rather trying in an informal conversation.

"Listen, boychik," she began, trying for a lighter tone, "scientists, even archaeologists, don't test theories. They test *hypotheses*." The blank look on her nephew's face showed that the distinction was not clear, so she continued in what she hoped was not an overly teachy manner.

"Stop me if you've heard this one, but science is nothing more than a way of organizing what you know about a subject so that you can understand it better. If you're going to use the **scientific method**, you have to put all your assumptions on the table, be explicit about the relationship between what you want to know and your method for finding it out, and be willing to be wrong. The scientific method means starting out with an idea about why something is the way it is—a *theory*. Then you come up with a number of explanations (called *hypotheses*) that you can apply to the facts of the case. Then you see which fit and which don't."

Sean frowned. "But everyone's entitled to their own opinion, aren't they?"

"Sure. But we use the scientific method to separate opinion—which can be based on faulty information, poor reasoning, or plain old personal bias—from ideas that can be verified. People have hopelessly ill-informed opinions about all manner of topics. The scientific method comes up with a conclusion you trust because you can follow the reasoning that leads up to it. Opinion is cheap. Scientific rigor is something else."

"OK, but you're really begging the question. Is archaeology a science or isn't it?"

"Perhaps I'm not answering because I don't like your question."

Hannah turned some of the bracelets on her skinny left wrist.

"This science or not-a-science business is a bit of a false dichotomy. Archaeology isn't a science in the same way that chemistry is. Listen! The scientific method works best when people can test their ideas by making predictions and seeing if things turn out the way they expect. A chemist can mix up a batch of chemicals under the same conditions several days in a row and predict that she will have the same end product every time. Archaeologists can make *some* predictive statements—that you will find sites next to water or even that the ability to create an agricultural surplus goes hand in hand with social complexity. But people aren't as predictable as chemicals, and they don't follow universal laws of behavior that we can use to predict—or should I say retro-dict—what they did in the past."

Sean stifled a yawn. He shouldn't have got her going.

"There are plenty who would disagree," continued Hannah, "but if you ask me, science is only a means to an end. Archaeologists like me use tools like the scientific method to approach questions that are essentially humanistic. We want to learn about people in the past who had real humanity and weren't just puppets whose strings were pulled by some immutable law of behavior, by the environment, or some other uncontrollable force."

ROLL CALL: Some of the Ideas in this here Book

ARE ALL FISH, BLUE FISH?

Using the SCIENTIFIC method we start with an idea, test it using systematically collected DATA, and REVISE the idea if necessary. Conversely, if we pull data haphazardly out of the Sea of Facts there's no way to know if what we catch is REPRESENTATIVE of what's really out there of if it's just a product of how we did our collecting.

Sean considered this for a few moments and found himself fairly satisfied. Or at least out-intellectualized.

"All right, Dr. Science, but who comes up with the idea, the theory, in the first place? Is *that* part of the scientific method?"

"Not at all. There's no big book of archaeological research questions that only PhDs are allowed to peer into at midnight on the full moon. It doesn't matter much *where* the original idea comes from so long as it's interesting. And you can actually get at it using archaeological data. In reality, research questions often come from a combination of things. Like the archaeologist's own interests, and what people are writing about in the professional journals and talking about at conferences like this." Hannah gestured toward a group of tweed jackets who were busy nodding and gesticulating to each other over by the coffee stand.

"So it's just a matter of fashion?" said Sean. "Don't archaeologists ever find out the truth? This year the environment explains everything, but next year everyone is looking at genes for the big answer. Is that it?"

"Now don't be glib, Sean. And don't forget the immortal words of that great, if fictional, archaeologist, Indiana Jones: 'If you want the Truth, try the philosophy department.'"

As he was inclined to do when a conversation turned overly highbrow, Sean rolled his eyes. "And just what does that mean?"

"Only that archaeologists don't claim to have the *one and only answer*. In fact, most often we don't come up with what most people would call an 'answer' at all. Mostly it's enough to contribute to the *understanding* of an issue without believing that we have to arrive at the ultimate cause behind some historical event or social process to justify our research. But to get back to questions, often they come out of some peculiarity in your data that you want to explain."

"Such as?"

Hannah fiddled some more with her bracelets, and they jingled softly. She needed a good example. Something simple but clear. Over by the coffee pot, an acne-afflicted young man and a middle-aged woman in regulation black aprons were refilling the matching wicker bowls with little packets. White for sugar, pink for Sweet'N Low.

"Remember when you and your mom visited that site I was digging over by Markleyville?" It had been two years since Hannah directed the field school on that Midwestern site, and she hoped that her nephew recalled the place. Sean had been more interested in studying the after-hours social life of archaeologists in the field than in studying their daytime doings.

The nephew smiled slyly. "I remember thinking that archaeologists are big on parties."

"Which I'm sure had no influence on your choice of career," replied the aunt. "So, you remember the site had been partly excavated the year before by Ian . . . well, by another archaeologist, as our department's summer archaeological field school. He, this other archaeologist, had excavated several of these bowl-shaped depressions and found that each one was surrounded by a series of postholes. This showed that they had been buildings with walls and a roof. And a couple of feet under the floor in the center of each they'd found a human skeleton, formally buried with grave goods and all. Since there were almost no **artifacts** on the surface inside the little buildings, my colleague thought the buildings were burial chambers. Tombs."

"Sounds reasonable to me."

"Except that they looked *exactly* like what the local Native Americans were calling *pit-houses*—simple huts whose floors are dug into the ground."

Sean shrugged and thumbed through his conference program. "Perhaps they were wrong."

"Perhaps. But there are many peoples who bury their dead in their houses and then abandon them or burn them down. So why couldn't that have happened here? To find out for sure I put together a simple hypothesis. I reasoned that if they *were* houses, we could explain why there were no artifacts inside if they were regularly swept out. If the hypothesis was right, I predicted that we would find the domestic artifacts—the people's daily trash—adjacent to the building's doorway. To test the hypothesis, we excavated a broad area of the ground's surface outside each building." She paused for dramatic effect.

Sean looked up from the program. "And?"

"And as a matter of fact, we found what we expected. The ancient ground surface was littered with potsherds, fragments of food bones, and other good stuff. So my hypothesis survived the test. You see, by focusing on the most dramatic remains, the other archaeologist missed the most interpretively useful part of the site. He went for the flash and ignored the substance."

Although to be fair, she conceded, the blame could be spread around. For their department chairman wasn't interested in spending precious funds on a discovery that amounted to a scatter of pottery and a few bits of old bone. That wouldn't attract more students to the department's underenrolled field school.

Nor, incidentally, did the discovery help Hannah to get a tenured position on the anthropology department faculty at Ennui State University when she came up for review the following spring. Undermining the professional reputation of one of your colleagues isn't considered the most effective strategy by which to gain his support. At the time of the vote, said colleague called in a favor and Hannah's bid for job security had to wait for another year.

That was her problem, she scolded herself. Too direct and combative. Too sure of herself, even when she was wrong. It was a piece of Israeli culture, like her contempt for waiting in lines, that had become part of her makeup in the five years that she spent in the country.

Hannah Green had made her *aliyah* (going up) to Israel at the age of twenty-two and had soon found a job as an archaeological monitor with the Israel Antiquities Authority. While many North Americans think of preserving the evidence of their country's history as a pastime for the overeducated and underemployed, in Israel archaeology and national identity are inextricably bound. Nationhood is quite literally a matter of life and death. And so it came to be that after two years of glorious freedom roving the country in a Jeep, Hannah found herself drafted into the army as a member of an occupation "essential to national security." In public, she admitted to being in the IDF Education Corps. But for the few in the know this translated to furtive, nighttime excursions into no-go portions of the West Bank and Sinai to check on the veracity of rumored discoveries by Jordanian and Egyptian archaeologists that periodically set the country buzzing.

After her service and a short but ultimately bitter romantic interlude that nixed her chances for graduate school in Israel, Hannah wangled a place at London's Institute of Archaeology studying the origins of agriculture in prehistoric western Europe. It was a long way from the Golan Heights to Ennui State University. But Hannah soon discovered that while politics are not pursued with such deadly force on campus as in the Near East, it isn't for lack of conviction.

Sean dropped his program, and it slid under the bench.

"Well, OK," he conceded grudgingly. "I suppose it makes sense. But that was a pretty simple hypothesis. How about the big ideas that supposedly make sense of everything? Everyone knows that archaeology can help us to date sites and to reconstruct how people lived in the past. But all those '-isms' and '-ists' that I had to memorize for my history of archaeology final? I never could see how they really help anyone to understand archaeology."

"And which '-isms' did you have in mind?" inquired Hannah over her steel-rimmed glasses. OK, so she needed bifocals. But she'd be damned if she'd get them.

"Oh, **Marxism, materialism, neoevolutionism, functionalism, postmodernism**." He rattled off the names in rapid succession. "The stuff that you're writing about in your book."

Hannah winced.

The draft of her undergraduate textbook, *Archaeology from A to Z*, was a long way from being complete, and she was working on her second time extension. Using Sue Grafton's successful alphabet murder series to structure an archaeological textbook had seemed like a good idea at the time, but the problem was making one theme build on the next. Of course, it was just a gimmick. But the question remained whether or not it was a gimmick that would sell.

She had no money to pay a real illustrator, and her hard-hearted editor insisted that authors pay the costs to use other published graphics. So Hannah was reduced to using her own artwork—a peculiar convergence of cartooning and Monty Python–like montage—to illustrate her words. Would Lascaux Press be amused? Who could say? The editor had warned her that a draft was due by July 22—or else. There was no need to complete the threat. It is well known in academia that would-be authors of archaeology texts are two a penny, and publishers jettison the flaky ones like yesterday's underwear.

"How about this?" offered Hannah. "If you give me the chance to show you how having a theoretical perspective is useful for understanding what happened in the past, I'll see what I can do about getting you employed for the summer."

He shrugged. "Why not? I've got nothing to lose."

So deeply had our protagonists immersed themselves in anthropological musings that neither noticed the figure that discreetly joined them. He stood halfway turned toward the conversationalists, his head cocked to take it all in. Dr. Ian Tuliver was a shortish man whose entry into early middle age had been marked by a heaviness around the waist and thinning hair that he swept directly back over his crown. In his early career the boyish visage had engendered certain extrascholastic yearnings on the part of more than one female graduate student. Recently he had developed a double chin that gave him the appearance of a debauched schoolboy.

"Doing a little after-class instruction?" inquired Tuliver. The innuendo belied his open smile.

Hannah sighed at her colleague's whine. Annoyed by the interruption, she acknowledged his presence by rising regally from her vinyl throne. At a shade under six feet, she had an advantage of four inches over Tuliver, who backed up into a concrete column. Yet the munificent smile remained on his chubby face.

"Am I to take it that your young *friend* is looking for work on an excavation?"

Sean was oblivious to what Tuliver was implying. He perked up and offered the haughty academic his hand.

"Because if he is," continued Tuliver, grasping the young man's hand with both of his own pink paws in a fair impersonation of a car dealer moving in for a sale, "if he is, I may have something for him."

Grinning and nodding like the village idiot, Sean assured the professor that he was very interested indeed. Oddly, Tuliver seemed to be more concerned with his colleague's reaction than Sean's. A tight feeling in her throat told Hannah that there was more to Tuliver's solicitousness than a desire to advance the career of a young man he had just met.

Yet Tuliver was strangely quiet when she asked about the site: Where was it? What was it? In reply to these and other mundane questions, the man would only smile and say it was an exciting and controversial site. All would be revealed, he said, if they would meet him later. Reluctantly, Hannah agreed—what else could she do with Sean bouncing around like a large puppy on the verge of a romp in the park? The time was set, more damp handshakes were exchanged, and Tuliver insinuated himself back into the sea of herringbone tweed and respectably faded Levi's.

One overpriced dinner later, the elder of our pair of not particularly well-fed archaeologists pushed the button for the fourteenth floor of the hotel. Their distorted images stared back at them from the elevator's reflective, faux-brass walls—on which Sean nervously drummed his fingers, creating small oily patches. The only other passenger got out on the thirteenth. She was an elderly woman whose eyes did not leave her shoes. As the doors closed, she turned and nodded at Hannah, touching the brim of her straw hat. Sean turned to grin at his aunt, who forced a smile in return.

Before dinner Hannah had taken off the heavy Southwestern-style necklace and changed into a severe, loose-fitting black dress and boots that added at least two inches to her height. Tuliver could be as slippery and manipulative as a politician. But whatever the **mamser** was up to, he would find Hannah Green ready for action and all business.

Room 1434 was near the end of a long, carpeted corridor, next to the soft-drink machine. The door was ajar, but Hannah carefully knocked on the jamb. She did not want to cause it to swing open, having no wish to catch her colleague in his unmentionables.

When another knock bore no fruit, she called out.

"Tuliver? Hello? Are you there?"

No reply. She knocked vigorously on the door, and it swung inward.

The aforementioned archaeologist sat—or rather slumped—in an overstuffed chair at the foot of the king-size bed. He clutched some papers tightly in one pale hand. His head was tilted at an unnatural angle and his mouth gaped open, as if caught in a scream. But he was silent, and his stocky form was profoundly motionless.

It appeared that Dr. Tuliver had received the ultimate critique.

"A" IS (ALSO) FOR ARTIFACT

In Which We Learn That Sometimes a Rock Is Just a Rock

With no more hesitation than if she were crossing the street, Hannah strode to Tuliver's motionless form and thrust two fingers onto his neck, probing for a pulse. The eyes fluttered, then snapped open. A familiar leer appeared on that pasty face.

"My dear Hannah, I didn't know you cared."

Smirking, Tuliver hauled himself into a more dignified position. He emitted an extravagant yawn.

"You really should learn to knock, my dear," he continued, "or someone might get the wrong idea."

Hannah kept her temper with an effort. The temptation to perform one of the more ghastly acts drilled into her by her military instructors was difficult to overcome. She heard herself ask what exactly Tuliver wanted of her.

"Nothing but your well-being, my dear," he drawled. "I just thought that you might care to give me a little help, a little collegial aid, on a piece of research that I have out in . . . well, out in the wild West, shall we say. There are certain, ah, aspects of the project in which you may be of use. And if all goes well, perhaps I could be persuaded to pen a short letter of recommendation to the dean. Naturally, I can't promise anything . . . but it could only serve to help with your tenure."

The desire to strike this grinning baboon was nearly overpowering. This was a clear quid pro quo. She was to help Tuliver out of whatever mess he had got himself into, and he wouldn't oppose her bid for tenure. But what was she to make of his coyness over the location of his site? Did he think she was out to steal his glory? Yes, the fool probably did.

"Suppose you tell me a little more about this site," Hannah said flatly. "Why do you need me? There are plenty of other archaeologists around." And plenty whose company he'd prefer.

"Well, my dear," said he in avuncular tones, "in this case you may have a particular expertise that is, ah, difficult to come by."

Good grief. Was that a compliment?

"My sponsor, you should understand, is a remarkably public-spirited man. He intends to develop the property containing this site into a retreat center. Not wishing to endanger it by his construction project, he has retained me to excavate it first. But I shall say no more of that until we have come to an agreement. Let us say that if you agree to spend the next six weeks at my site, I shall arrange for comfortable accommodations and a small stipend. Your duties will consist of nothing more than the occasional consultation. So you will have plenty of time to work on that book of yours. And your young friend," he turned and smiled generously at Sean, "I will employ as an excavator."

Hannah could feel Sean's eyes boring into the back of her head. No question what his vote would be. But the prospect of six weeks in the confines of a dig with Tuliver was not how she had anticipated spending the summer.

While Hannah wavered, Tuliver dug into his coat pocket and drew out a ziplock bag containing several small, gray objects—potsherds by the look of them—and tossed it to her. She fished out the fragments and turned them over one by one, inspecting the body and scraping each broken section with her thumbnail to assess the hardness of the fabric. Hannah shrugged. She'd seen a ton of them.

"Typical Neolithic types. About five thousand years old, give or take. This one's a piece of Peterborough ware. You can see the impressed decoration made by a length of twisted cord. They're all over England and Wales. And these guys are called Grooved ware because, well, they're decorated with incised lines. We found a bunch the season I worked for Guy Sieveking at the **Grimes Graves** flint mine site. These sherds are rather abraded. I'd say they've knocked around on the ground's surface for a while."

She glanced up at Sean, who appeared completely out of his depth, then looked directly at Tuliver.

"Sorry to disappoint you, but there's nothing unusual here. So I repeat, what would you need me for? There are dozens of archaeologists in western Europe who could identify these types of pots for you."

The professor smiled his crocodile smile. "Nothing unusual, are they? What if I told you these pots are from a site in, ah, North America? Would *that* pique your interest, my dear?"

And so it came to pass that Sean Doyle got his wish.

Washington State wasn't exactly Southern California, but it was a helluva lot closer than Illinois, and that was plenty good enough. He pushed the button that reclined his seat, causing the nearly empty juice can on the tray table behind him to wobble, overbalance, and drop to the plane's carpeted floor. Sean smiled a contented smile born of his good fortune and three cans of Budweiser, which, at twenty-four thousand feet, were having a pleasantly soporific effect.

The uneasiness that he had felt during and after their interview with Dr. Tuliver was dissolving. So what if he was a little secretive about the site? He had the right, Sean supposed. Hannah was making far too much of it. He glanced over at his aunt staring vacantly out the window at the ocean of clouds rolling to the horizon. As she sat, Hannah played with one of her long curls, wrapping it around a finger, then pulling it out like a spring. She was always brooding about something, he observed. Even the plane fare that Tuliver had generously offered them had set her off.

"You think I'm making a problem out of nothing?" she had demanded. "When was the last time an archaeologist paid your airfare? Never. You know as well as I do that contract archaeology projects are run very tightly."

"Except this one," Sean pointed out superfluously. "But isn't this the way archaeologists used to get money back in the old days? From rich guys? Maybe Dr. Tuliver's sponsor is just generous. Seems as likely as the conspiracy theory that you're cooking up."

"Back in the old days, huh?" she smiled. "Yes, you're right. But the game was very different then. There were only a few professional archaeologists in the early twentieth century. Most were university teachers, and the rest worked for the larger research museums, like the Smithsonian or the Field Museum in Chicago—places that have research departments and aren't just there to put up displays. In the very early days, archaeologists couldn't just apply to the government. They were expected to rustle up some of their own funds. So they'd go and make their pitches to learned societies and wealthy individuals, drink a lot of tea, and smile a great deal more than they felt like."

Sean closed his eyes and clasped his hands behind his head. Another two minutes, and he'd be out for the count. "Sounds like a bunch of politicians raising campaign funds."

"I suppose there's not that much difference. Think of the greatest discovery of the last century: Tutankhamen's tomb. Where do you think that the English archaeologist Howard Carter got the funds to run the project? From Lord Carnarvon, a wealthy man who just wanted to be part of a great discovery. And he was! Even as late as the 1960s, there were only a few archaeologists working outside academia in North America. Some worked for the National Park Service, and others for outfits like Colonial Williamsburg, where they helped reconstruct building plans from the colonial era."

"And then **CRM** was born," whispered Sean.

Hannah jabbed him in the ribs with a bony finger, and Sean jerked to attention.

"Yep. Cultural resources management. Just after the war—that's World War II to you, kid—people started to notice that development had created all these environmental problems. The air and water were polluted, and entire species were almost extinct. Well, someone, somewhere figured out that a lot of archaeological sites were being destroyed by the same processes of construction and intensive farming. Archaeology became one of the resources that had to be studied before a construction project could be approved.

"Laws like the National Environmental Policy Act and the **National Historic Preservation Act** were passed. They forced anyone who needed federal money or approval to look for sites that might be affected by their project, to see which were important enough to be saved or studied further, and to dig important ones that couldn't be protected."

Sean laughed out loud. "Yeah. I've heard NHPA called the 'National Archaeologists Full Employment Act.'"

"Well, it certainly increased the demand for archaeologists. I once read that over 90 percent of archaeologists in the United States work in the CRM field."

"CRM *industry*," he corrected. "The commercial archaeology firms even have their own trade association to look after their interests in Washington."

"Really? I didn't know that. Just like the Beef Council. I suppose they have a lobbyist, too. Call me old-fashioned, but somehow the idea of archaeology as an industry makes me cringe. Maybe it's because I'm totally out-of-date."

"No," said Sean, "it's because you already *have* a job."

Google Maps claimed it was about an hour's drive from Seattle-Tacoma International Airport to the small town of Vickiesburg. There, according to Tuliver, they could pick up the ferry to their final destination, Dougal's Island. Sean slept for most of the trip, reclining at nearly full length on one of the plush rear seats of their rented van. Hannah had not wanted to impersonate a suburban mother and her teenage son, but the silver and blue family wagon with the sliding door was the last drivable vehicle in the lot. According to the woman at the Hertz counter, a national convention of well-heeled university deans was in town and had cleaned out just about every rental vehicle in the airport.

They approached Vickiesburg on a narrow and not particularly well-maintained road that followed every turn in the Salmon River. Occasionally a rock slide would cut the town off from the world until the guys in orange from the DOT maintenance station over by Tacoma came to doze the boulders into the canyon below.

The road climbed to a wide, midslope terrace and made a broad turn to the east where the Salmon spilled out into the turquoise water of Puget Sound. Almost immediately, the van began to pass a flurry of buildings whose mixture of tourist schlock shops and boarded-up fish packers intimated that this was not a town in the midst of a boom. Thinking that a ferry was most likely to be found on water, Hannah turned down onto a steep road that forked to the left before a hand-painted sign advertising the volunteer fire department's annual pig roast (only $10.50 and $5.00 for kids!).

Although there was little resemblance between his grease-encrusted coveralls and the sharply pressed uniform of the model in the brochure on his counter, Rick McDonald of Rick's Chevron and Marine Supplies was

Vickiesburg's Hertz representative. He accepted the van with a nod and a question about what the pair planned to do now that they were stuck with no transportation at the end of the road. The ferry schedule on Rick's notice board confirmed that the craft was due to leave at 5:00 p.m., calling at three islands and returning to the harbor at 9:00 p.m. Rick was also the ferry service's ticket agent. He sold them two round-trips to Dougal's with the advice that they might as well buy both ways since there was no other way of getting off the godforsaken place.

The ferryboat *Island Maid* had a small glassed-in section ambitiously labeled "The Lounge" with a snack counter and half a dozen vinyl-topped tables and chairs screwed to the floor. Eventually the *Maid*'s diesel throbbed a little louder and a couple of deckhands strode purposefully about loosening lines and ignoring passengers.

While Hannah ambled over to the snack bar to weigh the merits of plain M&Ms and those with peanuts, her nephew flipped through an article on the Neolithic pottery industry. Soon he was deep in the arcane realm of rim forms, shell tempering, and surface burnish. It took three long coughs and an "ahem" before he raised his eyes and realized that a man had taken the chair opposite him and was trying to attract his attention.

He was an old guy, at least in his forties, Sean judged, although his hair was thick and dark. His half smile revealed a lifetime of dental neglect, while his generic jeans and garish T-shirt proclaimed him a careless shopper.

"Couldn't help seeing what y'all was a-reading," he began, glancing at the article in Sean's hands, "and I knew that you had to be a archy-ology student. Am I right, or am I right?"

Without waiting for a response, the yellow-toothed one held out his hand.

"Name's Claude. Please t'meet you."

Sean nodded lightly and shook the man's bony paw.

"I'm a archy-ologist myself, in a kind of a way," Claude went on without a pause for breath. "Always had a interest in picking up stuff, arrowheads and such, ever since I was a kid. Got a whole bunch of them set in acrylic in the coffee table back home. Real pretty they are." He picked up Sean's discarded article and flipped through the illustrations.

"These ain't much to look at, are they? Now, Al and me—Al, that's my boy—Al and me, we found these . . . well, these arty-facts. And they're something *real* special. Got 'em with me right here if you want to see."

From an old green canvas bag that had once held a French soldier's gas mask, Claude brought forth four lightbulb-size objects, individually wrapped in white toilet paper decorated with tiny blue flowers. Carefully, he unwrapped each object and placed it on its own bed of tissue in front of a puzzled Sean.

"Pick 'em up, why don't you?" said Claude gleefully. "Just look at that workmanship!"

The stones were gray and waterworn. They may have been basalt, but Sean had slept through physical geology and said as much.

The other puffed. "That don't matter, son. Look at the inlay work. Look at them figures. Look!"

Sean rolled the first of the pebbles over in his hand. The stone was crisscrossed with veins of some white material that could have been quartz. It was harder than the matrix that encased it and had not eroded as rapidly, leaving a delicate tracery of milky lines. In frustration, Claude jabbed at it with a long finger.

"There, look. Don't you see the old man with the beard? And that looks like a horse."

According to Claude, each stone showed a scene of mythical creatures, women with flowing hair, or armed warriors. They were clear evidence of a lost civilization, he said. Or a way overactive imagination, thought Sean. But not wanting to seem dismissive of Claude's claims, Sean turned the rocks over in his hands, trying his best to see the figures among the random lines. Eventually by concentrating on some elements and ignoring others, he could make out some of the fantastic creatures, although it occurred to him that the process would go faster with the aid of a few beers.

Now the discoverer of these amazing treasures bitterly told how he had taken the carvings to several universities and museums and was rebuffed.

"The fact is," confided Claude in a low tone, rerolling his hoard, "these so-called scientists ain't so open-minded as they pretend. The way

THE ROCKS O' MYSTERY...

Beachcombing on the Oregon Coast, Claude makes the find of a lifetime.

What might look like a bunch of ordinary pebbles are, on close inspection, intricate works of art.

Looking carefully he sees the forms of stately bearded kings and a beautiful princess with flowing tresses.

Perhaps, thinks Claude, these are the relics of a lost culture, a civilization that sank beneath the waves in an earthquake? Museums would soon be beating down his door and he could move out of the trailer down by the river.

On the other hand, they might just be a handful of rocks.

So what are they...

     rocks or relics?

I figure it is they just don't want to know about any discovery that might go against their own pet ideas, see. They spend their careers working up these theories and don't dare to think of other possibilities in case they're wrong. They've got a nice little club going, and they won't let no one in who don't agree with them."

He nodded significantly and tapped the side of his nose with a skinny forefinger.

"But there's one guy I heard about who's digging over on Dougal's Island . . ."

Sean returned the gesture with theatrical emphasis, wondering what kind of a loony tunes project he had got himself attached to.

The *Maid* docked at the end of a long, wooden pier that jutted out from the base of Dougal's granite cliffs.

It was after six o'clock, but the northern sun sailed quite high over the horizon. A deckhand dropped the steel ramp, loosed the chain, and signaled to those who were about to disembark. First off was Claude. With a cardboard suitcase in one hand and his precious canvas bag over his shoulder, Claude loped rapidly down the hundred-foot or so length of the pier and disappeared among the jumble of sheds and boathouses at the island's only deepwater harbor. As she followed him with her eyes, Hannah noticed a small form partly secreted behind one of the sheds. The figure nodded to Hannah and touched the brim of its broad-brimmed hat before slipping out of sight behind the rickety building.

Sean shouldered a mountaineering backpack that extended a good eighteen inches above his head. It looked overbalanced and ready to pitch him into the bay. A suitcase on wheels and a laptop computer case constituted his companion's luggage.

"Your friend seems to know where he's going," commented Hannah, hoping that she would have as much luck with Tuliver's directions to the excavation's headquarters.

Sean exhaled noisily. "Hey. I didn't notice you helping me out with that . . ."

He didn't know how to characterize Claude and left the sentence unfinished. "I'd never have guessed that you were so interested in fire extinguishers."

"It's always best to be prepared, you know."

"And you were prepared to leave your sister's son alone with the Rock Man."

Hannah stopped to disengage one of the wheels of her luggage that was wedged between two planks.

"Think of it as part of your archaeological education, Sean." She yanked the wheel free with a jerk, and they strolled on down the pier. "What was he talking about, exactly?"

"Mostly about his rocks. And you know, the more I looked at them, the more I could see the designs he was talking about."

"So do you believe that the figures are really there, or has he just convinced himself that they are?"

The young man scratched his head thoughtfully.

"Weeeellll. All the lines he pointed to are real. It's just that there are a bunch of *other* lines as well. And he's ignoring those. I guess I'd say the designs are there, but he created the figures by picking out the lines that make them. I suppose old Claude has decided what he wants to see in the rocks and is ignoring everything else. Like **Erich von Däniken**, who looks at carvings of the ancient Maya wearing fancy headdresses and thinks that they've got on space helmets. And that it proves spacemen visited the earth and taught the people how to build the Pyramids and those big carved heads out in the middle of the Pacific."

"Rapa Nui island. Yes. I guess von Däniken just can't believe that non-Europeans could have the brain power or the organization to build monuments like those. He certainly overcomplicated things. Generally it's best to look for the simplest explanation, as the more layers of speculation you add, the more likely you are to make a mistake. It's an ancient principle called **Occam's razor**.

"Of course, it doesn't always give you the right answer. But think of it this way: I hear a crash of breaking glass in my backyard. I go back there and find you holding a baseball bat. There's a broken window and a baseball among the glass. Now, it's possible that the ball dropped from a passing jet, bounced off the fence, and flew into the window."

"Possible but not likely, you mean," said Sean.

"Exactly. Science doesn't deal in certainties, only probabilities. Archaeologists dig up the end results of events and processes—like the broken window. We hypothesize about the causes, but we *can never know them* in the same sense that I know a sequence of events I experienced directly. Being wrong is part of being a social scientist. Not that we enjoy that aspect. But we know that while some types of knowledge are cumulative and build on previous discoveries, some of the models we are attached to now will end up on the scrap heap in a few years."

"OK. But what about something like the theory of evolution? That's a theory, right? But everyone treats it as if it were a fact."

"Evolution is one of those theories that has so much evidence on its side that we treat it like an established fact. But in that way it's no different from many other aspects of life. Listen. We drove down here in a van, right? Did you look under the hood to see if there was an engine there? Course not. We assumed there was and carried on as if it was there because all we wanted to do was get to the end of the road. All our observations of the van—how it sounded, the fact that it took us where we wanted to go, every interaction we had with it—were consistent with our belief that there was indeed an engine under the hood. It's the same with the theory of evolution. It's consistent with just about every observation we can make about the natural world. So we act as if it's true even though we can't prove it to be true."

Sean nodded thoughtfully.

"When you put it that way, evolution will always be a theory regardless of how much evidence there is in its favor. But back to old Claude. I don't believe his story about the unicorns and all that junk for one second, but some of what he said made sense. You say being wrong sometimes is just sort of expected. OK, I understand that. But it's like Claude said. Think of someone who's made his career and reputation on some idea. He taught it to his students, published articles on it, and generally carried on as if it was true. Now, you can't tell me he is going to shrug and say, 'OK, it was all for the sake of science' when someone comes up with a theory that is a better fit with the facts. It's just not human nature. No way. He'd fight for his ideas any way he could. And if that's true of an individual, wouldn't it be even more likely if the new idea threatened the careers of a whole bunch of people?"

Hannah put down her bags and smiled at her nephew.

"These are good questions, Sean. But if I talk and carry these bags at the same time for much longer, my arms are going to fall off before I run out of breath."

Brushing the loose rock from the top of a low wall, she sat and thought about her reply.

"You're asking another good question, boychik. Is archaeology self-correcting? That is, if an idea turns out to be wrong or someone makes a discovery that changes everything, will the profession accept it? Or would some kind of conspiracy develop to hush it up? Did I get it right?"

Sean had dropped his pack and sat on the ground leaning against it. He nodded in agreement. He felt uneasy about taking Claude's part in the argument, but the guy did seem to have a point.

"You'd have to be pretty dumb," Hannah continued, "to think archaeologists have some kind of priestlike devotion to *the truth* with no concern about their own welfare. We're just people, after all. We go to the dentist, worry about the future, and paint our kitchens. By the same token, we like to be right and don't enjoy being told when we're not, any more than the next person. It's as hard to generalize about us as any other group. So when Claude says we're all out for ourselves, it's about as accurate as saying all doctors order unnecessary tests for their patients because that's how they make their money."

"Some probably do, some don't. That's fair enough. But how does it *really* work? In the archaeology field, I mean."

"You want to hear a story? Sure, I can manage that." Hannah repositioned herself on her makeshift seat and began.

"Once upon a time back in the 1930s, there was this young archaeologist. He taught at the University of New Mexico and was quite a character. Handsome, smart, charismatic. All in all, a guy with a promising future. One hot summer he and his students were off digging **Sandia Cave**, a prehistoric site out in the boondocks, and they made a series of truly spectacular discoveries. The kind of things that get one cited in all the right scholarly publications and turn a small-time academic into a celebrity. He found a collection of artifacts he claimed were as much as twenty thousand years old.

"Now, this was long before the Clovis and Folsom cultures that supposedly crossed the Bering Strait about twelve thousand years ago. The Sandia artifacts were unique, and one even looked like a European type of spear. Nothing like them had been found before, and nothing like them has been found since. This guy's reputation was set. And, for a while, all the new archaeology textbooks and articles mentioned Sandia Man. It became as much a historical certainty as Clovis and Folsom."

"Since I've never heard of Sandia Man," ventured Sean, "I would guess that something went wrong."

"And you'd be correct. Soon the whole story started to unravel. And here's how it happened. When this archaeologist did his excavation, **radiocarbon dating** hadn't been invented, so there was no way to date artifacts exactly. When scientists came up with the method in the early 1950s, everything changed. Let's just say that questions arose about where exactly the 'Sandia' samples that this archaeologist sent in for analysis actually came from."

Sean's eyebrows shot up. "Are you saying the guy faked his data?"

"I *didn't* say that," said Hannah with great emphasis. "But after the problem with the carbon dating, other archaeologists began to reexamine the Sandia artifacts. Some seemed genuine, but others looked like recent pieces that had been reworked. I heard that one appeared to have been ground down on a grinding wheel!"

"Wow!" exclaimed Sean in amazement. "So he *did* make it up."

"I'm not going to speculate on that," said Hannah, "because we'll never know for sure. But I'll tell you one thing that brings us back to your question. If you take a look at scholarly articles on North American prehistory from the 1950s onward, you'll find that fewer and fewer mention Sandia as the years go by. And the ones that do tend to waffle about its authenticity by calling it 'controversial' or 'anomalous.' It took a while, but archaeology corrected itself. Not by publicly trading insults or destroying careers, but by simple attrition."

"You mean," translated Sean, "that they ignored it and it went away. Which is exactly what *we* should do unless you want to spend tonight on the beach."

The evening wore on, and even in those northern latitudes the sun could not be expected to linger above the horizon indefinitely.

Hannah fished out the directions Tuliver had printed in small, precise letters on a used envelope. As instructed, the pair took the packed-gravel road inland. Turning at the first gate, they left the paved surface. The trail was primitive, and the suitcase on wheels bounced and snagged in the

rutted surface. They paused at the top of the rise, and while the aunt rested on a boulder and dug a piece of gravel out of her shoe, Sean dumped his pack and scrambled up a rocky outcrop.

From this vantage point, Dougal's Island was revealed as a rolling piece of real estate, mostly covered with a softwood forest that opened up here and there into broad, wet meadows and divided down the center by a range of rocky prominences. Their path led east around one such meadow, then through a gap in the hills.

The shadows were long now, and the line of rock ahead looked almost like fallen castle walls, battlements that had crumbled either from an attack or from the decay that comes as the natural partner of old age. Here, in the failing light, it wasn't so hard to visualize the mythic civilization concocted by Claude the Rock Man. Sean scanned the long outcrop, noticing how the shadows built doorways and battlements. How a half-fallen pine draped with hanging moss took on the look of one of Tolkien's ent creatures. How a trick of light created the impression of a human form spread out on a large flat rock near the base of the hills.

Sean leaped from his perch and with long strides took off across the meadow like a sprinter. Focusing on a pair of towering rocks that flanked the figure, he charged through the meadow's boggy interior, soaking his boots in mud that smelled of earthy decay. At the far side of the bog, he slowed, less sure of himself or what he might find. Would it be an injured climber? Or just a pattern of rocks?

Or, lying perfectly still and clothed in pure white, the most awesomely beautiful girl he'd ever seen. Her eyes opened. She raised herself on one delicate elbow and spoke with the voice of a cooing dove.

"And just what the hell are *you* staring at, goon boy?"

Sean was in love.

CHAPTER THREE
"B" IS FOR BINFORD

In Which We Learn What's New about Archaeology

"**A**re you dumb as well as ugly?" demanded the Vision.

On some level, Sean was aware that he was being questioned. But somehow he couldn't wrench his attention from how the failing sunlight lit up the red-blond hair that poured in ringlets over the young woman's shoulder. Freckles had never looked so good.

"Well?" She clipped his shoulder hard with the heel of her perfect hand. He staggered backward, tripped over a moss-covered boulder, and sat heavily and with little dignity on the gravelly ground. His T-shirted arm raked across the rock's jagged surface and tiny lines of blood oozed from the surgically thin, parallel scrapes, forming droplets that ran down his elbow. Not that Sean noticed. He opened his mouth but could only come out with a series of throaty noises.

Meanwhile, the Vision had pulled her lovely self upright and swung her legs around so that they hung over the edge of the flat rock. She slipped her feet into a pair of sandals and stood up, hands on hips, glaring fiercely at Sean, who lay in his pile of confusion, tiny rivulets of blood streaming down his elbow into the dirt.

"I . . . ah, didn't . . . ," he burbled. "I didn't mean to . . . I thought you were . . . someone was hurt or something."

"Well, I'm not," she said fiercely. And then, seeing less danger and more slapstick in her rescuer's position, she backed up to a crooked frown.

"You can get up now," offered the Vision. "Just stay over there." Sean shuffled meekly to his feet and winced as he extended his bloody arm.

"Listen, I'm real sorry if I scared you," he began, picking a piece of gravel out of his elbow.

"Hey, goon boy, what gave you the idea I was scared?" she demanded. "You just surprised me, that's all. I was in a second-level state, or I would have heard you coming."

Now, Sean had no idea what a "second-level state" might be—nor a first-level, for that matter—and was about to ask, when a horn blast sounded from somewhere in the middle distance. The Vision's elegant head turned slightly to better hear the trumpeting sound. She bent to brush a few stray specks of red dirt from the hem of her robe.

"Gotta go," she said, and she clambered around the large, flat stone where Sean had discovered her. Turning, the Vision tucked some wayward locks behind her perfect ear and gave Sean the gift of a fleeting smile.

"I'm Freya," she said, disappearing into the rocks. "Don't suppose I'll see you again, goon boy."

"Now tell me again," insisted the aunt, "that you haven't been smoking that wacko weed."

Urged by an instinct that a sociobiologist might say was a desire to protect her kin group's genes, Hannah had made her way around the bog through which her sister's son had so recklessly scampered, to find him quite alone and bleeding.

"You must admit," said she, applying the first of a patchwork of Band-Aids to Sean's torn arm, "it's a pretty wild story. A beautiful goddess who dematerializes at the sound of the **shofar**."

Although it was hardly out of keeping with what she knew of Sean's romantic imagination.

"I didn't say it was a shofar. Just a horn. And she didn't disappear. She just sorta left."

Sean was hurt, and not only by the scrape on his arm.

But somehow neither his aunt's playful sarcasm nor her medical ministrations seemed to matter. He had been in the presence of perfection. And even in the Vision's rejection he found fuel for a fantasy of requited love.

The remainder of their walk to the dig's headquarters was uneventful, and the two kept their thoughts to themselves: Hannah was concentrating on Tuliver's directions, which were thankfully as precise as the letters of his tiny printing. And Sean was so distracted by his encounter with the Vision that he would cheerfully have followed his leader off a cliff, had she led them to one.

And so it was that the pair arrived at the imposing wrought iron gate and graveled driveway of the New Magick Retreat Centre—or the Summerfield School, as the chipped and blistered sign had announced for the last sixty years.

It is probably unnecessary to say much about Eugenia Rubicon-Bott, the late founder of Summerfield. The erudite reader will surely be familiar with that great woman's contributions to the education of girls. It is enough to mention that from 1905 until 1943, the school was well known in the most progressive circles for its programs in art, theater, and Jungian psychology. Shortly after the inconvenience known as World War II forced her to put up the shutters, the founder went into decline. Mrs. Rubicon-Bott was buried on her beloved island on Christmas Eve, 1943.

The old place was invisible from the road, hidden behind a dense yew hedge and a sweeping curve in the driveway. The wheels on Hannah's suitcase sunk into the loosely packed gravel. She dragged it unceremoniously, leaving a deep gouge like the spoor of a giant snail.

As the yew and lush privet bushes ended, our travelers emerged from the gloom and took their first view of the building that loomed ominously not forty feet in front of them.

"Wow," offered Sean, looking up for the first time in a quarter of a mile.

"Wow, indeed!" responded the aunt.

Dark and *rambling* were the adjectives that came to Hannah's mind. Deep, overhanging eaves and dark, shingled walls, over a half story of rough stonework. The facade was flanked by twin stone-built towers whose soaring topmost windows would have provided a spectacular view of the surrounding country down to the bay, had they not been tightly shuttered. Four wooden posts, their rough bark intact, supported a broad porch, and gave the impression that the roof had grown like the forest canopy from the trees themselves.

A prosperous building contractor, Henry Bott had constructed the place to the specifications of his dear Eugenia in the avant-garde Arts and Crafts style. The outside had never seen a lick of paint because, as Mrs.

Rubicon-Bott had declared in her now-famous dictum, "I will have no lying buildings for my girls. Wood shall look as wood and stone as stone."

"Wow," said Sean redundantly as they climbed the porch steps. A note written on the back of an envelope and taped to the door directed the senior of the two to her quarters. It made no mention of her companion.

"OK, so where do I go?" asked Sean of the door.

"If you're the new guy on the crew, you can follow me," came a bored voice from the shadows. A slight male figure rose from his seat on the porch railing. "I am Alasdair Crisp, the associate field director. Dr. Tuliver asked me to look out for you, and I've been waiting here since six thirty."

The welcoming committee was not amused, and it was clear that Sean had not just found his soul mate.

"We got a bit sidetracked . . . ," Sean began apologetically, but he was interrupted by their host, who flung open the door without a glance at either of the newcomers.

"Well, you'd better come this way," said Alasdair. He stalked inside. Sean looked at Hannah and shrugged.

"Guess I'll see you later. Perhaps," he added over his shoulder, "I'll get Mr. Happy to tell me where the kitchen is, and we can get something to eat." Now there was an idea.

"Fine. Let's meet at my room in a few minutes."

Ahead, twin staircases curved gracefully to a balcony. But Hannah did not go that way. Following directions and expecting the worst, she dragged her luggage into the wide hallway, through a pair of double doors, and into a large, bare room with a stage at the far end. Rock music pounded from a pair of tiny speakers attached to a battered CD player that sat on the edge of a table, just in front of the stage.

The archaeologist's quarters, said the note, was the right-side dressing room. Finding that the door to her abode was stuck, the new resident applied her shoulder. The door yielded on the second try. Hannah stumbled into the room and found herself face-to-face with a wild-haired woman moving rapidly toward her. Her adrenaline surged momentarily until she recognized her own image. From waist height to ceiling, the far wall was one continuous mirror, where student actors of past years had applied their makeup.

How absurd, she chuckled, to be scared by your own reflection. But such a face!

She glowered at herself and tried to pat down the ringlets. Buffeted by the wind on the crossing and curled even tighter by the ambient moistness of the Pacific Northwest, curls sprang like a halo around her head.

Small and windowless, but with the unexpected luxury of what a sign announced to be the door of an attached bathroom. This was better than Hannah had dared to hope, and she smiled in quiet relief. She rattled the door of the putative bathroom, found it stuck, and decided to try again later.

Now the intelligent reader may feel that others of our protagonist's age and status would have been less than pleased by such meager accommodations. And this your author will admit. But Hannah's standard of comfort was influenced by twenty-five years of military quarters and archaeological field camps, neither of which is much known for an extravagant regard for personal ease. With a bit of cleaning, thought she, the place would do just fine—although a real bed to go with the mattress would be a nice touch. Hannah hummed along as the CD player began booming out "**Purple Haze**," a familiar old Jimi Hendrix track.

Behind the door she found a makeshift clothesline consisting of a length of rope tied between two nails driven into opposite walls. The previous tenant had obligingly left a couple of rusty, wire coat hangers dangling there. The new resident appropriated them for her black, going-to-meetings blazer and a white cotton shirt that had survived the trip with minimal wrinkles because of their owner's skillful packing. Thinking the hangers were a little too rusty to use with her one respectable shirt, Hannah fished around for some clean paper in a promiscuous heap of debris left, no doubt, by the former lodger.

Among the torn and wrinkled posters, dusty membership fliers for some archaeological organizations, and grease-stained lunch bags was a one-inch sheaf of white paper held with a heavy-duty clip. She flipped the stack over and grasped its identity from the title page and blank signature line even before reading that famous line: "A thesis prepared in partial fulfillment of the requirements of the degree of Bachelor of Arts with specialization in Anthropology."

Now let it be known that nosing unbidden through the edited draft of a senior thesis is like reading the student evaluations of someone else's

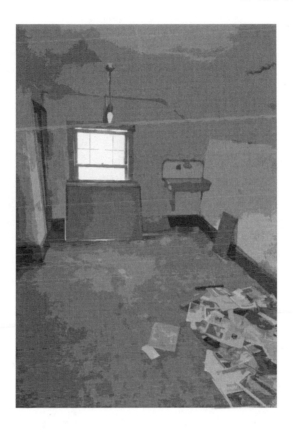

course. It's forbidden, but tempting all the same. But since this stuff had been discarded, there seemed no harm, and Hannah rationalized her nosiness as professorial curiosity. She quickly wished she had let it lie.

Underlines, double underlines, and exclamation points scarred the paper like wounds on a soldier's corpse. Every page was flecked with crimson marks. Some had margins full of commentary, tightly packed in tiny, precise capitals, calculated to pierce and tear like razor wire. Occasionally she came upon an entire paragraph slashed across its vitals with a stroke of the same angry red ink. Hannah tut-tutted with professional disdain. The manuscript hadn't been edited, it had been assaulted.

Hannah was hooked now and couldn't draw back. Sitting on the floor with her back against a wall, she opened the manuscript at random and began to read.

She was brought out from her reverie in a couple of minutes.

"Hello. Hello?" It was Sean, standing in the doorway holding a tray loaded with the requisites for a simple meal. "You know, I've been standing here for five minutes trying to get your attention."

"You have not."

"Well, a while, anyway. I've brought some food." He squatted down next to her and began to slice a loaf of crusty bread with a knife that was too small for the job. "Must be some hot article you're reading."

Hannah shook her head mournfully. "'Fraid not. Whoever wrote it doesn't understand much about the history of archaeology. Her advisor let her know about it, too. Brutal."

"You mean, like the **New Archeology** thing?" asked Sean through a mouthful of bread and cheese.

"You've heard of it?" She sounded surprised.

"Hey! I didn't sleep through *all* my eight o'clock classes."

"Just *some* of them, huh? OK then, Dr. Science, tell me all about it."

"Weeeeell," began Sean, suddenly deciding that his shoelace needed tying. "I guess this guy **Lewis Binford** thought it all up in 1962."

"Oh, is that right?" asked his aunt in a tone that intimated otherwise.

"Yeah, sure he did. I'm pretty certain of that much. He decided that archaeologists should be more like anthropologists, so he started this idea of the New Archeology. That's right, isn't it?"

As she often did when playing for time, Hannah rearranged the silver bracelets on her left wrist in order of thickness: the plain bracelet first, then the sand-cast Hopi one with the tiny piece of turquoise, and finally the cheap, wire ring that she had worn since she was a girl.

"Well, sort of."

She always began that way when she wanted to soften a no. Patting the manuscript, she continued.

"This writer felt that way too. But it's not that simple. It's like I've said before, archaeology isn't like Major League Baseball. It doesn't have a commissioner who can wake up one morning and decide to dump the designated hitter or extend the season by two games. It changes because the people who do it—the archaeologists themselves—decide individually that the change is a good thing. And, of course, not everyone goes along with the program. Some people stick to whatever they've been doing all along. Others take what seems useful to them—such as a particular technique—and leave the rest.

"Binford didn't just come up with New Archeology off the top of his head. It was a response to what had been going on in North American archaeology for the previous sixty years. He just said what a lot of people were thinking and suggested a new approach."

Sean nodded thoughtfully. "Yeah, I can see that. Anyone can whine and complain about how bad things are, but nothing changes unless someone comes up with an alternative. But what was so terrible about archaeology at that time?"

"That depends on who you ask."

"That's your favorite answer, isn't it?"

Hannah ignored the gibe. "Think for a minute about why people studied archaeology in the early twentieth century, when it was just getting a foothold as a legitimate discipline. It was about reconstructing culture history. Who was doing what and where, and when they were doing it. Archaeologists were kinda like historians with trowels."

"And even worse fashion sense."

"Thanks, I'll ignore that. What was I saying? North American archaeologists were mostly interested in reconstructing the sequence of cultures that lived here. And they were pretty successful. Think of the important techniques that were developed from the turn of the nineteenth century through the 1920s: controlled excavation, taxonomy, seriation, and so on. By the 1940s, archaeologists all over the country had defined distinctive groupings of prehistoric artifacts used by regional cultural traditions. Archaeologists understood the technology these groups used and how they made a living off of the land."

"Their subsistence practices."

"Right. In just one generation, these old-timey archaeologists had made incredible strides in reconstructing basic North American cultural chronology. The culmination was in 1939, when old W. C. McKern and his colleagues put several of these local sequences together to create the **Midwestern Taxonomic System**. And if it could be done for the Midwest, it could be done for the entire continent. It was a great achievement."

"Well, yeah . . . ," began Sean tentatively.

Hannah raised her eyebrows.

"The thing is . . . what more was there for these old archies to do? I

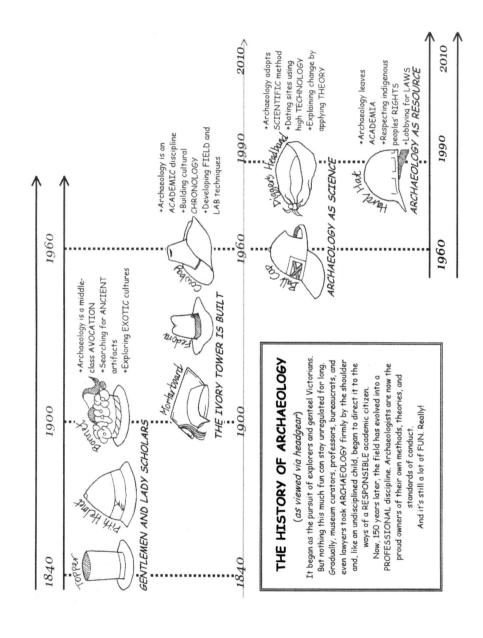

1840   1900   1960

Topper

Pith Helmet

GENTLEMEN AND LADY SCHOLARS

Bonnet

+Archaeology is a middle-class AVOCATION
+Searching for ANCIENT artifacts
+Exploring EXOTIC cultures

1840   1900   1960   2010>

Mortarboard

Fedora

Cowboy

+Archaeology is an ACADEMIC discipline
+Building cultural CHRONOLOGY
+Developing FIELD and LAB techniques

THE IVORY TOWER IS BUILT

1960   1990   2010

Belly Cap

Digger's Headband

+Archaeology adopts SCIENTIFIC method
+Dating sites using high TECHNOLOGY
+Explaining change by applying THEORY

ARCHAEOLOGY AS SCIENCE

1960   1990   2010

Hard Hat

+Archaeology leaves ACADEMIA
+Respecting indigenous peoples' RIGHTS
+Lobbying for LAWS

ARCHAEOLOGY AS RESOURCE

THE HISTORY OF ARCHAEOLOGY

(as viewed via headgear)

It began as the pursuit of explorers and genteel Victorians. But nothing this much fun can stay unregulated for long. Gradually, museum curators, professors, bureaucrats, and even lawyers took ARCHAEOLOGY firmly by the shoulder and, like an undisciplined child, began to direct it to the ways of a RESPONSIBLE academic citizen.

Now, 150 years later, the field has evolved into a PROFESSIONAL discipline. Archaeologists are now the proud owners of their own methods, theories, and standards of conduct.

And it's still a lot of FUN. Really!

mean . . . I know they were great and all that. But after they built their chronologies, what were they going to do next?"

"Ah ha!" Hannah poked the air with a gesture that made her bracelets jangle. Here was progress in the education of Sean.

"That, boychik, is the point. The old-timers could say that certain groups moved from one place to the next, established towns, developed complex societies, conquered one another. And they knew that these peoples got ahold of pieces of technology—such as the bow and arrow, which changed their tool kit almost overnight. So if you know all this, what more *is* there to know?"

"That's easy. Once you know what happened, y'have to work out why."

"Exactly. Up to that point, archaeologists had kept themselves pretty busy just describing *what* had happened in prehistory. If you had asked them *why* things happened, they'd have given you *historical* explanations and told you all about how ideas move from one group to the next by diffusion and conquest, and by people migrating from one place to the next. Think about this: Peoples all across the world, from Mexico to Mesopotamia, developed agriculture independently. Why? What did the places have in common?

"A few archaeologists like **Gordon Childe** said that local economic conditions determined the direction of cultural change. But most didn't think to ask if there were *general* processes—aside from particular historical conditions—behind change and innovation. It's the difference between seeing history as a series of more or less unique events and seeing it, like Childe did, as the predictable outcome of a set of social, environmental, or economic forces."

"Whoa! Hold up, Hannah," cried Sean, holding his head. "You're losing me there. What are these forces you're talking about?"

"OK, I'll try it again. You were right when you said that North American archaeologists were at a bit of a dead end by the 1940s. And that is when **Walter Taylor** came out with his book *A Study in Archaeology*. Many people haven't heard of it, but it predates your friend Lew Binford by fifteen years. Taylor said it wasn't enough for archaeologists to just *describe* what changes had occurred in the past. We had to *explain* them in relation to some process that is greater than any particular historical context. Taylor's approach was a type of functionalism. He saw culture—all aspects of culture—as a mechanism that enables people to adapt to their natural and social environment. Cultural differences, he thought, are essentially caused by subtly dissimilar adaptations to different environments."

"So he'd explain a war as . . . ?"

"A way for people whose population has grown too big to get more land."

"OK. So everyone started following him, did they?" asked Sean with lessening enthusiasm.

"Not at all. Until the Binfords—that's Lewis and Sally—published their *Perspectives in Archeology* in 1962, things went on pretty much as usual."

Sean stood up and stretched. There's only so much archaeological history a guy can take at the end of a long day.

"Hey. Mind if I try out your private bathroom before I go?"

"Be my guest. I couldn't get the damned door open earlier. Must be jammed."

Sean rattled the handle and pushed.

"That's strange. I think it's locked from the inside." He pushed harder now, but to no effect.

"Let me try before you break it down," requested the aunt. "It's one of those cheap, push-button locks. They're easy to deal with."

"Deal with?"

"Just watch and learn from your old auntie."

A few moments of rummaging in Hannah's bag produced a trowel worn thin by seasons of excavation and a steel nail file. Using the former as a pry bar, she jimmied the wooden molding away from the door frame.

"Hold this," she ordered her accomplice. "Yes, just enough so that I can . . ."

The nail file slid under the molding and bit into the latch. Carefully, Hannah worked the point back and forth until she had forced the latch back into the door. The staccato sounds of Jimi Hendrix's classic "Machine Gun" wafted in. Evidently someone had turned up the volume on the CD player.

"Done!" said the amateur locksmith. She pushed the door open and smiled modestly up at Sean. "Another of the little skills you can pick up in graduate school. Almost makes it worth the fees."

But Sean's amazement at his aunt's way with a jimmy was swept from his mind at the bizarre sight revealed through the open bathroom door.

A figure was balanced precariously with her left leg on the toilet and the other on the windowsill—in an attempt to climb through while struggling to hold on to a large, blue, plastic basket. She turned and giggled at the duo and seemed about to speak, when her sandaled foot began to slide inexorably around the slippery lip of the white porcelain void. There was a shriek as the bathroom bandit fell over backward and the contents of the laundry basket flew through the air.

Hannah stepped back and calmly folded her arms.

"Welcome," she deadpanned, "to the exciting world of northwestern archaeology."

"C" IS FOR CULTURE PROCESS, AND "E" IS FOR ETHNOARCHAEOLOGY

In Which We Learn How the New Archeology Grew Old

Hannah flipped on the light. The prostrate form groaned and pulled herself upright. She drew a thin hand across her face, smearing blood from forehead to cheek, and looked up at the two like a frightened child. Motioning Sean to stay where he was, Hannah approached the young woman and gently helped as she propped herself between the shower stall and the wall.

"Ohmagawd," said she, in an accent suggesting Southern California. "This is, like, *so* humiliating."

"You've cut your thumb on the broken window," said Hannah clinically, "but that's about all." The injured one sat meekly as the digit was bound in a wad of tissues. "Do you want to tell me what's going on?"

"This is, like, *so* humiliating," she repeated, cradling her bandaged hand.

"Let's collect your stuff and go into the other room," said Hannah. And they did.

"This is, like, *so* humiliating," said the girl, glancing up at Sean and then down at her bandaged thumb. "I was, like, just doing the last of my washing—this used to be my room, you know," she added. "And I heard you two. I was going to come out when you started talking . . ." She paused for a few seconds to summon up her courage. "Talking . . . about my thesis, and I just had to listen in. And, like, by the time you'd finished . . . it was way *too* embarrassing to show myself. This sounds, like, really dumb, doesn't it? So I thought I'd just climb out of the window. And then I slipped."

She gave a weak, hopeful smile and went back to looking at her bloody dressing.

"Ah ha," nodded Hannah. "So it's *your* thesis."

"That's right." The young woman smiled at Hannah and tucked some long, blond threads behind her ear. "It didn't sound like you thought much of it" she added.

"Not true," put in Sean gallantly. "I learned a lot about that New Archeology business from what you wrote, Sandy. It is Sandy, right?"

"Sandra," she corrected. "Sandra Beech."

"Of course."

Sean realized the significance of his mistake. In one very obvious way, Sandy Beech would have been quite perfect for this tiny, blonde Californian. But it did make you wonder what kind of people would have inflicted such a name on an innocent baby. Although Sean had once met an archaeologist called Warren Pease, who gleefully insisted that his literary moniker helped break the ice with women.

"Sorry I didn't recognize you, Sandra." Hannah hoped that this wasn't a student from one of her big lower division classes who had somehow been erased from her memory. "Ennui State isn't that big."

"Oh no, Dr. Green. I've never had a class from you. I was a transfer student. But I've seen you around campus. Everyone knows you're, like, a long-distance runner or something."

"Or something. You've been working with Professor Tuliver, I suppose?"

"Yeah. I kinda moved over to archaeology from cultural anthro to, like, get more hands-on experience. But it's harder than I thought. Not just gluing artifacts together."

She looked down and started rearranging her balled-up laundry in a halfhearted sort of way.

"Basically, there's only the senior thesis between me and graduation. I've just gotta finish it this summer. There's, like, this job, y'know? Starts in September, and they want me to have the degree by then."

"A job where you need a degree in anthropology?" said Sean in disbelief. "Sure you didn't get a concussion when you hit the floor?"

"Yeah, really!" Sandra pulled her head out of the laundry and smiled shyly. "I'm gonna be an assistant research specialist at Recreational Illusions. It's, like, an independent film company in northern California that made the movies about the archaeologist Indiana Joan. They're turning it into a TV series, and . . ."

". . . and they want you to play Joan," suggested Sean.

He couldn't help contrasting nervous little Sandra with the tough and buxom actress who, as Dr. Joan, had karate-kicked her way through miscellaneous evildoers and snake-infested jungles in the search for cool relics.

"Hardly! I'm going to help with the technical details. Make sure she doesn't say anything, like, really wrong from an archaeological perspective. That's why I chose the history of archaeology for my thesis." She glanced over at Hannah. "But Professor Tuliver just hates it. I just don't know what to do. And I really want this job. Really."

For most people, sitting on the floor discussing the history of archaeology with a woman whom one has just found flat out and bloody in one's bathroom would be a strange concept. But adaptation to changing environments has been an important theme to archaeologists since the 1930s. And what the hell, thought Hannah. It would be a good way for the girl to regain some of her lost dignity. They could take care of the blood later.

"Well, you did make it sound like the New Archeology just appeared out of nowhere," Hannah said gently. "In your thesis, I mean."

"I guess I never thought that it was too relevant to, like, what's going on now. I mean, the early archaeologists weren't really even anthropologists."

"And 'archaeology is **anthropology** or it is nothing,' right?" quoted Hannah.

"Er, I'm lost," chimed in Sean.

"So let's go back to the ideas behind the New Archeology, OK? First, you should realize that the New Archeology wasn't just one thing, one standard approach that everyone grabbed at the same time. Archaeology is full of people with their own ideas and more than a few iconoclasts. No one was going to just sweep through and *make* everyone give up on their old ways of doing things overnight. Or even in a generation. The New Archeology was very influential, but it didn't lead to everyone using the same methods or theoretical approaches."

"Then what did they have in common?" asked Sean.

"Mostly that they were dissatisfied with the direction the field had been going in. What people like Taylor and the Binfords did was to get the field fired up with the idea that it was possible to create an anthropology of the past. That archaeologists weren't and shouldn't be satisfied with knowing *what* happened in the past, they should ask . . ."

She waited expectantly.

"Er . . . why it happened?" said Sean tentatively.

"Right! So the New Archeologists had this important new goal, and they looked to the hard sciences for the techniques to make it happen. You remember that radiocarbon dating had revolutionized the field in the 1950s. So archaeologists wanted to know what else these guys had up the sleeves of their white lab coats. And you also have to think about the culture of the era. Post–World War II America was in awe of science. We'd put men in orbit, invented plastic, eradicated polio, and put a TV into everyone's living room. Americans felt that science had all the answers, and many archaeologists . . ."

". . . who—with the possible exception of Alasdair Crisp—are members of human society, felt the same," said Sean.

Sandra giggled and put down the T-shirt she had been folding.

"Right," continued Hannah. "So we dipped into the scientists' bag of tricks and came up with useful tools. Like the hypothetico-deductive method and statistical analysis. The New Archeologists also weren't too happy with the supposedly unscientific way that archaeologists connect the data they dig up with their interpretations. Common sense, they reasoned, doesn't apply across cultures. My interpretation of the distribution of artifacts on a site shouldn't be shaped just by my experience as a modern human. And it certainly wouldn't be the same as that of someone who lived in a hide tent two thousand years ago. So the New Archeologists concluded that we should study living people and see how they use and discard artifacts. Then we could take that as an analogy to interpret what we find on archaeological sites.

"That's how **ethnoarchaeology** was born, and for a few years hordes of graduate students with clipboards went tracking nomadic tribes all over the place. Binford himself lived for a while up in the Arctic with the Nunamiut, studying how they used caribou bones. Ethnoarchaeology was the beginning of what Binford called **middle range theory**, which is really just a way of bridging the gap between what archaeologists find and the behavior that created the stuff."

Sean exhaled noisily. "The Eskimos must have thought Binford was nuts."

"Probably. It's an occupational hazard if you spend your time picking through other people's garbage. But Binford didn't watch the Nunamiut schlep bones around in the snow just to see how *they* did it. The Nunamiut are only one case of a group with a certain cultural adaptation. What Binford wanted to do was extend this particular example to cover all hunter-gatherer groups in the past, so that he could better understand the real meaning of the remains they left behind. Binford wanted to generalize."

"You mean, like, he wanted to make vague statements?" asked Sean, shaking his head. "Why would he want to do that?"

"No. What I mean is that he wanted to come up with statements about human behavior on the same level as the natural laws that hard sciences are based on. Generalizations in the sense of statements that are true of all peoples everywhere. At least, those who are at the same level of technological and social complexity. Essentially, he was looking for the laws of human behavior."

Sean nodded. "Yeah, I've heard that before. But I've never understood how you could come up with a statement that's always true. I mean, people are so . . . different."

"That's right." It was Sandra. She had kept her head down through most of Hannah's monologue, picking at her bandage and tucking the ragged ends under the sides. But now, remembering her own breakthrough on this point, she became almost excited.

"It's like this. As individuals, people are, like, unique. But anthropologists aren't much interested in individuals, they'd rather look at whole societies. A lot of anthropologists start out with the idea that all the practices that make each culture unique are ways people have developed to help them adapt to their environment. If you accept that, then it makes sense that groups who live in similar natural environments are going to develop ways of meeting the same challenges that are similar at some deep level. The behaviors are different on the surface, but they serve the same purpose: to help the people make the best use of their situation. What was it that Kent Flannery said about the New Archeologists? They weren't, like, interested in the Indian behind the artifact, but the *system* behind both the Indian and the artifact."

Hannah nodded.

"Try that again," said Sean. "You guys lost me back at the systems."

"What Flannery meant," said Hannah, "was that these archaeologists weren't interested in studying *what* individuals or even whole societies did just for the sake of describing them like an ethnographer does. They wanted to explain how the entire suite of cultural practices and artifacts is part of an integrated system that helps the society adapt to its environment. They were seeing human beings as just another part of the planet's ecological system."

"Yeah. **Cultural ecology**. I sorta remember it," nodded Sean. "So the New Archeologists were into that, huh?"

"Sure they were. The idea had been around for a long time, but the New Archeologists picked up on it because it *explained* things. The model was based on the idea that there's a clear unequivocal force that shapes all cultures. Cultural ecology said that cultures aren't just random conglomerations of social relationships, customs, and beliefs. Instead, each one is uniquely structured to maximize people's efficient use of their natural environment."

"OK, but if every culture is so well adapted, why do they change? I mean, why should they?"

Hannah and Sandra both began speaking at once.

"By feedback," went on Hannah, the winner.

She pulled out her notepad and, while they spoke, drew one of her odd diagrams in which figures in robes and pointy hats were nudged in various directions by little arrows labeled "population pressure" and "food surplus."

"If an innovation—irrigation, say—is more effective than the old way of growing crops, then the folk who use it will grow more, put away more of a surplus, and increase the number of people who can survive the winter. So their population will grow, and the new technique will spread, and so on.

"And don't forget," Hannah went on, "that past a certain scale irrigation needs someone in authority to organize digging ditches and to coordinate how the water is distributed between family plots. So before you know it, you have an entrenched social hierarchy. At least, that's what the 'irrigation hypothesis' claims."

Damn you, Lew Binford!
These anthropologists are driving me NUTS

ETHNOARCHAEOLOGY
or
LEW AND THE ESKIMO

An archaeologist digs up a 5,000-year-old stone artifact and says, "*This is a projectile point, an arrowhead.*" How can she be so confident? After all, she wasn't around when the object was made and, being dead, the person who used it isn't likely to volunteer much information on the subject.

The answer is ETHNOARCHAEOLOGY—studying modern people who have similar technology for clues about how folks in the past used and disposed of their artifacts.

Lewis Binford is a pioneer in the field. He spent portions of four years living with Nunamuit Eskimo watching how they processed bone into tools. It's true; I swear! Anthropologists are quite an... interesting bunch.

Binford noticed that small fragments of bone accumulated in a "*drop zone*" around the workers, while they threw larger pieces either in front or behind them into what he called a "*toss zone.*" Working on the assumption that people in the past had similar habits, the intrepid anthropologist used this information to interpret the distribution of artifacts around 15,000-year-old fire hearths at an archaeological site in Pincevent, France.

"Cultural ecology wraps everything up in a neat package, doesn't it?" said Sean.

His aunt grinned and gave Sean a look as if there was more to be said on the subject.

"Yes. And if you'll take my advice, you'll be careful of explanations that seem to account for everything. Cultural ecology is a powerful theoretical model. But it is *only* a model, a story about the way the world works. Like any other explanatory model, cultural ecology can be quite deterministic."

"Deterministic?"

"Yes. **Determinism** is the idea that a given set of conditions will always result in a certain outcome. It works in chemistry, but people . . ."

". . . are just too unpredictable."

"Correct. Sometimes a random event that has nothing to do with adaptation will change the course of culture history. For example, the army of Ghengis Khan had swept across Asia in the twelfth century and was ready to invade Europe. They were unstoppable. Then Ghengis died, and his armies got recalled. What if he had kicked off a month later? Would we be speaking Mongolian now instead of English? Would the Industrial Revolution never have occurred? Or the Enlightenment? Would the Pilgrims never have sailed to North America?

"Take it from me, no model explains *everything*. But the New Archeologists made us face the fact that without a model or an approach, we've no place to begin, no way of orienting ourselves to the problem . . ."

". . . or even knowing what the problem is," laughed Sandra.

For much of the night Hannah's bony thighs were gouged by the steel springs that stuck through the ancient mattress. She had flipped the thing over and found that the back side was even worse. Finally she folded her blankets into thirds, put them on top of each other, and slept on the pile, like the heroine of "The Princess and the Pea."

At exactly two minutes before six, Hannah woke and stretched out her left arm in an arc, encountering the alarm clock at about forty-five degrees. By the use of an uncannily accurate internal clock, Hannah was always—or nearly always—able to beat the thing to the punch. Crappy

DETERMINISM AND THEORY

A **DETERMINIST** takes the position that specific, identifiable factors 'determine' the direction of history and culture, as well as individuals' roles in society. For example, **RACIAL** determinism (a form of racism) holds that an individual's culture or personality is determined by their 'race'—the physical characteristics that distinguish one population from another. It's hard to see how anyone who has visited a multi-ethnic society could possibly believe this, but many do.

Although human culture must, in the long term, help people survive in their physical environment, **ENVIRONMENTAL** determinism emphasizes adaptation as the ultimate creator of cultural forms and practices. People are viewed as just another organism that must survive in a hostile habitat. You can think of Karl Marx as an **ECONOMIC** determinist because he saw all human history as resulting from conflict between social classes.

It's OK to divide the world up for the purposes of study and analysis. After all, we have to categorize influences before we can evaluate them. But to really **BELIEVE** that human history is driven by a particular force is to deny people a role in influencing the course of their own history and their own lives. It's useful for social scientists to study the world **AS IF** our models of it are true, but we shouldn't believe that any theoretical scheme can have all the answers.

night or no, she would run three or four miles that morning as she did at home.

Bracing herself against the porch, Hannah stretched out her hamstrings. Left leg first and then reaching up and around in a half circle, bending to grasp her ankles. Last, she pushed the ever-present silver bangles up her forearm to avoid clanking bracelets while she ran. A thick layer of cloud—probably ocean fog, she thought—drifted low across the sky, barely skimming the treetops. Occasional wisps curled down near the ground, twirling in mad spirals until they exhausted themselves, condensing against evergreens and undergrowth. It was just as well that she had put her pale gray tracksuit over the stretchy top and thin, nylon shorts. Generally that was all she needed at this time of the year to run a couple of circuits along the creek at Ennui State.

Had she looked up at the shuttered tower window as she ran off, Hannah would have noticed an elderly woman nodding several times in her direction and gently touching the brim of her straw hat in salute.

The runner chose a well-trodden path that might take her in the direction of the waterside, and padded along at an easy warm-up pace. Running a new route is a whole different experience from doing a familiar course, Hannah observed. You have to concentrate. There are decisions to make (like which way to go), so there's less chance of slipping off into that familiar meditative reverie as the legs pump, the arms swing, and the breath keeps time.

Hannah covered a couple of miles through the evergreens and emerged onto an open coastal terrace where the trail split, giving her the choice of heading either down toward the water or back into the trees. She stopped, breathing heavily, hands on hips, and looked out over to the bay. A stone-built tower, perhaps a lighthouse, sat on the headlands. It was really very picturesque, and Hannah had made a mental note to check it out at some time during her stay when a flash of light caught her eye. Someone was over there with a pair of binoculars. Or, as the sergeant in boot camp would have said, perhaps a rifle with a spotting scope. She dodged back into the trees and watched for more glints that never came.

Dumb paranoia, scolded Hannah.

She ran on, more annoyed at her own disproportional reaction than its cause. Hannah had noticed this heightened awareness before, and sometimes it was mighty inconvenient. But there was something about having been shot at during her time in the army that had left her with a residual alertness that had no sense of geographic appropriateness.

Distracted and no longer enjoying her jaunt, Hannah was just beginning to consider turning back when she tripped and barely saved herself by stumbling off the trail and into the brittle limb of a dead pine tree. A long welt began to rise at her left forearm, just below the bracelets, and Hannah swore extravagantly as she rubbed her injury. She turned to grab the object that had ambushed her so effectively and lob it into the next century, but she hesitated. It was a very familiar item: a wooden pole, three feet in length, marked off in alternating black and white stripes.

She seized the stick. "You're a goddamned photographic scale," said she in surprise and consternation.

Wisely, the stick made no response. Its restraint was rewarded by being tucked under the arm of its captor, who continued to run in the same direction.

Now, it doesn't take a New Archeologist applying the hypothetico-deductive method to predict that where there's an archaeological scale, there's an archaeological site not far away. Such was Hannah's expectation, and it was confirmed after a couple of minutes of running.

Ahead, the trees gave way to a small clearing, perhaps five hundred feet across, dominated by a low mound and a huge rock. A single, half-dead pine sapling had managed to get a foothold on the rock's surface. The piles of fine screen that fanned out from its base suggested to Hannah that the tree was only a temporary guest, doomed one day to tumble to the earth as its unsteady foundation collapsed from under it.

The signs of an archaeological excavation were all about, though not so different from a construction site to the uninformed. To the right was a sad-looking trailer, surely the site office. The boxy structure had once been the home of a family of tourists who had unaccountably abandoned it on the island in 1988. It still bore stickers from a dozen states, and one showing the owner's membership in the Good Sam Club, that testified to its former life on the open road. A few steps to the left, a twenty-foot-long former army tent sheltered what was probably the artifact lab. Shovels, picks, and other digging tools had been placed without much care against a wooden rack outside the tent, while two or three overturned wheelbarrows and several dozen white plastic buckets formed a heap around a nearby pine stump.

Hannah was in mid-harrumph at the unprofessionally promiscuous pile when she saw the first of the upright stones nosing through the pine needle carpet. Scrambling up the pine stump, her eyes ran from one stone to the next as they circled the mound. A long rectangle about four feet wide had been outlined in yellow string from the base of the great rock toward the center of the mound, and a few inches of soil, the results of the excavation, had been piled haphazardly on either side.

"What the . . . ," mumbled Hannah as she jumped down and approached the excavation. "This isn't . . . right . . . ," she added, stooping down to retrieve a piece of rough, black-surfaced pottery from the back-dirt pile to which she supposed it had been assigned by a less-than-observant student.

Somewhere between shock, delight, and disbelief, Hannah made her way from one upright stone to the next. It was as if she hoped to learn from these mossy surfaces how symbols of an ancient European culture found themselves in an island pine forest half a world away. Hannah leaned upon a stump and considered how inconceivable it all was. No wonder Tuliver had been so secretive. If the site was what it seemed, the professor would be an overnight celebrity.

Hannah had stood for a couple of minutes staring up at the back of the great rock and musing over these various paradoxes when she heard the crunch of boots on dry forest cover approaching the clearing. She checked her watch. It was only just past seven, far too early for the excavation crew to arrive. Tuliver hadn't taught an eight o'clock class in years, and Hannah thought it unlikely that he metamorphosed into an early riser while in the field. In no mood for conversation, Hannah slipped behind her stump.

"Do keep it down," pleaded the first voice. "If Dr. Tuliver were to find you here . . ."

He left the sentence hanging, but it was clear that the result would not be pretty. There was a familiar nasal quality to the man's speech in which Hannah recognized Alasdair Crisp, her unfriendly greeter from the previous evening.

"I knew we should have come out earlier," hissed the voice.

"Now don't you worry, lover," came a woman's self-assured response. "But just for the record, as I recall it was you who couldn't get his little ass out of the sack this morning."

There was some giggling, followed by a significant silence and what sounded to Hannah like a hand swatting the back of a pair of jeans.

"There'll be plenty of time for that later," the woman's voice cajoled. "But right now, suppose you get your hand outta there and tell me all about this great discovery of yours. Hmm?"

"It's sweet that you're so interested in archaeology," said Alasdair smugly. Ian Tuliver had an apt student in this one, thought Hannah.

"Yeah, ain't it? Now, about the site here . . . it's from the Stone Age?"

Alasdair snorted contemptuously. "Hardly. The idea of Stone, Bronze, and Iron ages is quite primitive. Although the general public"—he used the phrase as if it were synonymous with *idiot*—"still clings to it."

The woman ignored this sneer, and Alasdair continued in full teaching assistant mode. Hannah could visualize the little snot pacing, Tuliver-style.

"The **Three Ages** were devised in early nineteenth-century Europe," he lectured, "to classify sites according to the type of materials found there. At the time, archaeologists thought that human societies evolved through a universal and immutable set of stages, from simple to complex, and that the use of stone, bronze, and iron tools corresponded with these stages.

"Of course, now we know that is all nonsense," continued Alasdair, as if he had personally authenticated the fact to the scientific community.

"Just think of the Indians in this part of the West. In only a couple of generations, they went from using stone tools to iron ones, without using bronze at all. Of course, it all happened through the process we call 'diffusion'—the way ideas and artifacts spread from one place to another. That must be how this site came to be here," Alasdair offered vaguely. "Every indication is that it's from the Neolithic. Could be as much as five or seven thousand years old."

"Post–Bandkeramik period, then," said his companion quietly. But Alasdair in full lecture mode didn't seem to hear this scholarly aside.

"The European Neolithic," he continued, "is the period when societies made an increasing use of domesticated crops and livestock, with a concomitant drop in emphasis on wild resources. Populations grew and became more settled. The trend started about eight thousand years ago, somewhere in southeast Europe, and took one thousand years to get to western Europe and Scandinavia. Archaeologically, we see a widespread use of pottery and ground stone for grinding grain crops, as well as large-scale pieces of engineering such as causewayed enclosures, burial mounds, and megaliths."

"Like Stonehenge, you mean?" asked the woman in an innocent tone, which Hannah thought odd considering her recent under-the-breath comment. "I went there once. The slaughter stone gave me the creeps. I heard there's a place around here where the Indians made human sacrifices and ate them."

"Oh Patty, you are a silly girl," laughed Alasdair as if correcting a five-year-old. "Those are just stories. No one knows what Stonehenge's so-called 'slaughter stone' was used for. But this site"—and here his voice became breathless with excitement—"is really something different. There's never been anything like it found in North America. It's shaped like a western European chambered tomb—there's likely to be a burial under that mound—and it has Neolithic pottery that has been authenticated by an eminent specialist, Dr. Hannah Green."

Hannah stiffened at the mention of her name. This was why she'd been invited. No doubt Tuliver planned to rely on Hannah's reputation to support his claims when the inevitable questions arose about the site's authenticity.

"What we desperately need," continued Alasdair, "is a carbon sample so that we can date the site. But that's going to be difficult to find because the acidic soil in this damned pine forest would have eaten away wood and bone in no time. Our hope is that there's charcoal or a cremation at the center of the mound. For these materials," he declared with all the authority of a second-year graduate student, "would have survived the millennia."

Hannah had had as much as she could take of Alasdair's pontification. As the student's oddly attentive girlfriend pressed him for more details, Hannah slipped quietly behind the cover of the mound, intending to slink out into the woods. But taking one last glance back at the great rock, she stopped in midpace.

"Now I know I'm dreaming," she gasped. For there, carved into the face of the great rock, was an anthropomorphic figure with the faded but unmistakable protuberances of the female form.

"It's a goddamned Neolithic goddess."

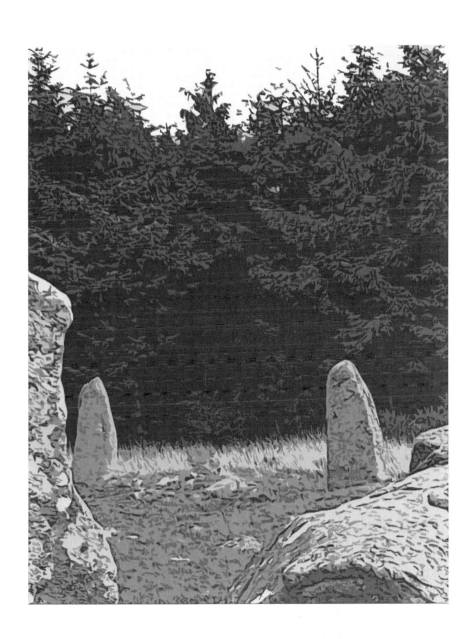

"D" IS FOR DIFFUSION

In Which Dr. Green Goes from Diffusion to Confusion

Hannah's head was still swimming three hours later when she and Sean were escorted around the site by Tuliver.

Her problem, of course, was how a figure with an odd resemblance to the famous "god-dolly" from the five-thousand-year-old Bell Track site in England came to be carved on a rock in Washington State. What was next—an Egyptian sarcophagus? None of it made any sense, and yet here she was looking at the evidence.

It didn't take much acting to convince Tuliver that all this was new to her. How could she not be amazed, confused, and excited even at a second view?

"I just don't know what to say."

"I know, I know!"

Tuliver's round face was beaming with pride at the opportunity to show off his site to a colleague. The students, who had been sworn to silence, were only students, after all. They couldn't really be expected to understand the magnitude of the discovery. But the awe of a colleague was something to savor.

"Isn't it just spectacular?" he gushed in great glee.

The three stood near the point where Hannah had first seen the stone circle and just stared for a full minute.

"Now come and see what's on the other side of the entry stone," said Tuliver, breaking the silence. "You won't believe this. It's . . . it's . . . unbelievable!"

He bustled the visitors to the eastern side of the rock, and flung his arms open like an artist displaying a completed work.

"Well? What about this, then?"

The little man grinned and nodded his head rapidly. He glanced back and forth between his discovery and Hannah, as if to observe both her reaction and its source.

"I believe I'll call it the Washington Venus," he announced.

"Why not the Tuliver Venus?" suggested Hannah.

"Do you think so?" Tuliver reflected a long moment before giving his judgment. "No, that would be a bit too much."

Back in her room, Hannah tried to evict the Venus de Tuliver and everything associated with it from her mind and replace it with a matter of immediate concern: "D for Diffusion."

Oddly enough, the words of the obnoxious Alasdair Crisp had set Hannah's mind to the task of making this concept palatable to your average undergraduate stuck with a general education requirement. On a piece of yellow lined paper, she sketched out a model showing an odd little creature clutching a hammer and leaping over similar individuals. She sat down to convert the thought into words.

And yet the things Hannah had seen that day wouldn't stop creeping into her thoughts. There were basically two ways in which Hannah could account for the site on Dougal's Island: either it was a product of the infusion of ideas from Europe at some point in the distant past, or it was the independent invention of these cultural forms by Native Americans. Or, in archaeological lingo, it was a case of either **cultural diffusion** or **indigenous invention**.

Crisp had been quite right about the concept of diffusion—the spread of ideas and artifacts across space and time. It *had* undermined the simplistic nineteenth-century notion that societies must go through a sequence of technological advances that build on previous stages. Isolated groups had been known to move from simple technology to computers in only one generation, as they came into contact with people from the outside world.

It was not so much the invention of an idea or a tool that changed the world, but rather the way it spread and the way it was adopted by others.

Take the bow and arrow. It wouldn't be true to say that one day about fifteen hundred years ago everyone in North America was using *atlatls* (spear throwers), and the next they were shooting arrows. And, as a matter fact, atlatls never did go out of use. But knowledge of the bow spread faster than any other prehistoric innovation that archaeologists could document. As soon as arrow points appeared in a region they became ubiquitous, and since the tip of an arrow was much smaller than a dart or a spear point, it was easy for archaeologists to recognize. The arrow point was what archaeologists called a *horizon marker*—an artifact that diffused widely and rapidly.

Hannah tried her hand at drawing a truck with a cowboy behind the wheel, thinking that the automobile would be a more familiar example of a horizon marker. Not so good. She'd stick to arrows.

Since they were unique, the stone circle, the carving, and the rest didn't constitute an archaeological horizon in Washington State. So one possible explanation was a single contact by Europeans that had not lasted long enough to influence local Native American culture.

That's not entirely inconceivable, she thought. For it wasn't so long ago that historians laughed at the idea of an eleventh-century Norse colony in North America. Now it was a demonstrated fact, with plenty of hard archaeological evidence. It seemed that the Norse settlement in Newfoundland only survived for a couple of generations and had no lasting effect on the culture of the native peoples. There had been no diffusion of ideas or technology out of the community.

Even the long-held view that North America was settled exclusively by people who skipped across the land bridge from Asia about twelve thousand years ago was being rethought. Respected archaeologists were now saying that there might have been several immigrations in the deep past—perhaps including people from Europe. The oldest human remains in North America, such as the 9,400-year-old bones of a man from Spirit Cave in Nevada, didn't look like modern Native Americans at all. Presumably his people were either absorbed into the dominant population or died out almost without a trace.

OK, so why couldn't there have been a European colony right here about five thousand years ago? Hannah asked herself.

Because, came the reply from her skeptical side, *it's a hell of a lot farther to Europe than it is from Newfoundland, and—in case you'd forgotten—there is no Northwest Passage, so they would have had to walk the whole way.*

And surely indigenous invention wouldn't explain the site. This one seemed particularly far-fetched. The idea posited that unless there was hard evidence of contact with other groups, a group's culture—and this included its *material* culture—developed by its own independent invention. It was the radical alternative to diffusion as the explanation of cultural differences and similarities. Was it possible that a native North American group independently developed so many of the traits of people from the European Neolithic?

Conceivable, she supposed. *But incredibly unlikely.*

But the most improbable explanation of all came from the principle of limited possibilities. This idea started with the observation that some problems have a limited number of practical solutions. For example, just because people in India and Guatemala used flat slabs of rock to process cereal grains into flour, we shouldn't assume that the resemblance came about because of diffusion or culture contact. After all, how many ways *were* there to grind seeds? But the same couldn't be said for art and design. Every region on the earth and at every period of history had its own vernacular architecture and art. There were any number of potential ways to use rocks and mounded soil to create a monument, as there were virtually unlimited styles of carving.

So much for limited possibility, she thought.

Hannah was no closer to explaining the site through any of these archaeological concepts. Nor, incidentally, had she made much progress persuading "D for Diffusion" to materialize on the page.

Eight hours of sifting soil through a one-quarter-inch shaker screen, with virtually nothing to show for it, had cooled Sean's enthusiasm for this particular site.

Yeah, he knew that it was unique and all that, but finding an artifact once in a while didn't seem too much to ask. There was stuff on the surface all right, but nothing in the mound itself. Digging would have helped break the monotony, and he rightly felt that he could move more soil than Terry Jones, his diminutive partner. But there was no way he was going to annoy her by making that suggestion. Especially not in hearing distance of the Neanderthal-like creature who was hanging around Terry's portion of the trench, apparently for no other reason than to smile shyly at her.

Alasdair had called the young man Big Dave, for obvious reasons.

Sean didn't like to stare, but he was quite a specimen. Big Dave had the broadest sloping forehead that Sean had seen outside of an anthropology textbook, and his more than three hundred pounds were poured into a frame about six feet tall. The effect was a barrel on legs.

"You shall work here with Theresa," Alasdair Crisp had announced that morning after Sean's site tour was over. "If you have any questions, I'll be in the office. You'll find this nothing like those CRM salvage digs that you're used to—this is a research excavation." He zipped his turquoise jacket against the wind and turned toward the sanctuary of the site office.

"Biting sarcasm," murmured Big Dave. "Way humiliating."

Sean wasn't clear on Alasdair's meaning, and said so to his partner after Alasdair had stridden away. Both CRM and research seemed to involve digging holes in the ground, taking notes about the soil layers, and making sure not to mix artifacts from different **proveniences**.

"Do they have a-holes like him in charge of CRM projects?" Terry asked. "Maybe that's the difference."

Sean laughed. "Is he really so bad?"

While Alasdair had been speaking Terry had been vigorously, even viciously, scraping the ground. At their introduction, she had given Sean only the briefest of glances. Now she sat back on her knees and fixed him with a hard glare, made more intense by severely short, blue-black dyed hair that framed her sharply pointed jaw. Terry pulled a kerchief from the back pocket of her jeans and, workmanlike, wiped the sweat from the back of her neck.

"That jerk," she growled, and Sean recoiled almost physically at her vehement tone. "He has no idea what this site is about. Did you know he's only a second-year grad student? The moron couldn't dig his way out of a kitty litter box. There are plenty of people on this site who've had far more field experience than him. But the Lord High Tuliver likes his fancy manners because they impress that capitalist running dog who claims to own this site. It's frikkin' feudal, the way he runs things here."

His conservative upbringing had left Sean unprepared for this sort of emotional outpouring. He mumbled something noncommittal and, when Terry released him from her gaze, dumped a bucket of soil in the shaker screen and immersed himself in his labor. Sean decided not to suggest that they trade off digging. They did not speak again for at least half an

hour, by which time Big Dave had ambled off to some other part of the site like a giant herbivore searching for new pasture.

By the end of the day, Sean was bone tired. Since he wasn't permitted to actually set trowel to ground, he had screened soil for the excavators. This involved running up and down the trench with thirty-pound buckets of soil all day. Meanwhile, Tuliver's grad students had considered the significance of subtle soil changes, and Alasdair had loudly questioned whether or not the dearth of artifacts was the result of "the new kid's" inability to recognize them.

Sean plunked himself down in a wheelbarrow, closed his eyes, and wondered where the nearest cold beer was located. With his luck, it was probably back on the mainland. If it hadn't been for the chance meeting with the goddess yesterday, this job would have been a dead loss. He smiled just thinking about her, and slowly drifted off to sleep saying her mysterious and beautiful name.

Freya . . . Where are you, Freya?

It seemed to Sean that he had only dozed for a few minutes when his world turned upside down. Someone had flipped his couch, and he found himself sprawled on the ground looking up at . . .

"Hey, it's you."

"Yep," replied Freya, ungoddesslike in camouflage pants and T-shirt, but with a delicate circle of green vines around her head like the crown of a wood nymph. "And now we're even, goon boy."

Sean lifted himself onto one elbow and grinned.

"Seems like I'm always looking at you from this angle. Kinda suitable, you being a goddess and all."

Furrows appeared on Freya s brow.

"Don't you say that. Specially so close to Her." She cocked her head toward the great rock. "Get up now."

She offered Sean a hand, and he was surprised by the strength in that slim arm. And also by the fact that she retained his dirty hand in hers for a few moments longer than was strictly necessary.

"I always come here at this time. After the archaeologists have gone home," she explained, gently. "This is a holy place for us. Come on, I'll show you."

"Us?"

"The Children of Odin."

"Oh, I see," said Sean, not seeing anything at all, but following all the same.

"Our camp's over the next ridge at the old lighthouse keeper's shack. We came up from northern California on Wednesday to make sure you archaeologists weren't harming Her." Freya's voice was light, and she spoke in a singsong that captivated Sean to the depths, as they say, of his being. "We could feel the vibrations. We knew something was wrong."

Before he knew it, Sean heard himself mumble, "There's a disturbance in the Force, Luke."

But if Freya heard him, she gave no indication. They walked on around the string-enclosed excavation trench to the east side of the great rock.

"There she is," said the girl reverently. "Freya, my namesake. Isn't she beautiful? Isn't she just out of this world?"

Sean drank in the features of his companion's perfect profile.

"Sure is," he said with so much feeling that it was obvious even to the worshipful Freya that he was not talking about the stone image.

Rather abruptly, she turned and demanded, "What's your name?"

"Sean Doyle."

Freya seemed relieved. "That's Irish, right?"

"Yeah. My dad's folks were from there. Though my mom . . ."

"Did you know," she continued, "that the Irish race is made up of the descendants of Joseph through his son Manasseh?"

Sean recognized this as some kind of biblical allusion but didn't give it much thought. The analytical part of his brain was rapidly shutting down, and the romantic lad was all emotion and senses. To be alone with Freya toward the end of the day, to be the object of her attention, the one for whom that silky voice spoke. He had to concentrate hard just to keep up the illusion that he was following her conversation.

They backed away from the great rock and unknowingly sat on the same pine stump that had supported Sean's aunt that morning when she had heard a very different sort of conversation.

In soft tones, Freya spoke of the ancestors of the ancient Angles and Saxons, the invaders of Britain, and how they were descended from what she called the "lost tribes" of Israel. She told how this group had wandered northern Europe for centuries, and how the historian Tacitus had reported in his book *Germania* that the Germans of the time (who, together with the Scandinavians, went on to invade the British Isles) held that they were descended from an individual called Mannus—which, of course, derived from Menasseh.

"Of course," agreed Sean.

"Now Machir was the son of Menasseh," continued Freya, "and his son was Gileath, the father of the Galadon of North Wales, the Galadi-Galatians of Gaul, and the Caledonians of Scotland. And his son—Gileath's, that is—was the ancestor of a group of Saxons called the Haeferingas, whose name we see in the town of Havering in southeast England."

Now Sean was not so smitten that he didn't realize something weird was going on here. But Freya seemed so authoritative and enthusiastic—and she was sooo beautiful when she was all wound up—that he let it go.

Everyone had their quirks, he supposed. Why shouldn't Freya's thing be ancient history?

"So these folks made it over to North America, you think?" said he, trying not to sound skeptical.

"Oh yes. You archaeologists have found plenty of evidence. Hebrew inscriptions on stones in a so-called Indian mound in Newark, Ohio, and lots of other things." She waved her hand to suggest the evidence was of such a quantity as to be beyond enumeration.

The Newark Holy Stones? Uh-oh.

The case was all too familiar to Sean from an archaeology class. It seemed that years ago an amateur archaeologist found a pair of stones engraved with Hebrew characters in an Ohio burial mound. One turned out to be a version of the Ten Commandments. The only problem was that they were written in Modern Hebrew, not the language of the ancients. It was quite clearly a fraud—probably commissioned by a local Episcopal priest—although some groups who wanted to "prove" their own versions of history still pointed to the stones as hard evidence of ancient Israelites in the New World.

Fine. But how did you tell the girl with whom you intended to spend the rest of your life that her philosophy was based on bogus research?

"I've heard," he began cautiously, "there are some problems with the Newark Stones."

"Such as?"

"Well, you know how cultures have distinctive styles of artifacts that archaeologists can trace through time? Well, the styles of the Newark Stones are nothing like any other ancient Israelite artifacts. They're unique."

"And that's a problem?" There was an edge to Freya's voice now.

"Well, archaeologists like to have more than one line of evidence," he began gently. "If the Newark Stones were genuine, wouldn't there be other artifacts that looked like them back in the Near East somewhere? Like something in a similar style?"

Freya shrugged.

"Don't see why there should be. You archaeologists are always looking to find fault with other people's ideas. But you can't deny Her."

Freya nodded toward the great rock.

Well, that settled it. There was no way Sean was going to pursue this line of argument. It had occurred to him to bring up alternative interpretations of the so-called goddess images: Like Alice Kehoe's suggestion that some of the Upper **Paleolithic** carvings that archaeologists and others routinely said were breasts could just as easily be male genitalia. Especially if you suspended them using the holes that were bored in one end. Or the idea that rotund figures like the famous Venus of Willendorf might have been made by women themselves, recording the stages of pregnancy.

Realizing that absolute honesty only gets you so far in a romantic relationship, Sean kept his ideas to himself.

"Now you have to leave."

Freya's words jerked Sean out of his trance. The fantasy of walking his lovely goddess home through the evening woods evaporated like mist in the Dougal's Island morning.

"I have to serve Her, you see."

Freya glanced up at the figure, then turned to Sean and gave him the lightest peck on the cheek. He was still in shock when she stood up and, arms above her head, walked serenely toward the great rock with more grace than Sean would have thought possible in anyone wearing army boots.

Somehow, "D for Diffusion" had been outlined, had taken shape, and was now safely filed away in some cybercranny on the computer's hard drive.

Hannah closed her notebook and stood to stretch the abused muscles of her back. The clock said a quarter to six. Still fifteen minutes before the scheduled crew reception, which meant that she should leave immediately. For as Hannah well knew, if you put archaeologists within striking distance of free food, it disappears faster than sand through a quarter-inch shaker screen.

Guaranteed.

The tall woman in the long black dress with too much clunky jewelry caused no more than a raised eyebrow as she entered the converted classroom and immediately began piling comestibles onto a paper plate. Each of the crew of four had either seen Hannah on the site that day or had heard, at second or third hand, how enthusiastic she was about the project and how certain, how very certain, she was about the absolute undeniable authenticity of the discovery.

She looked around for Sean. Strange to find him absent when there was food to be had. There was the blonde Sandra, sitting in an institutionally straight-backed chair nibbling on corn chips doused in salsa. Behind the door, the unstoppable Alasdair Crisp lectured Dave, the young Neanderthal whose eyes kept creeping to the television where the San Francisco Giants were concluding a three-game sweep of the Dodgers. Or perhaps he was more interested in Terry, who was following the game from her perch on the arm of an overstuffed couch.

"There you are, Green. Come and meet Mr. Bott."

There was no mistaking the voice, or the awful familiarity with which Tuliver slid his hand under Hannah's elbow. He eased her over to the side of the room, where a grizzle-bearded man of about fifty was sitting in what must have been the room's only comfortable chair. When he rose to greet her, Hannah was surprised to find herself overlooked by at least three inches. And she in her boots, too!

"Mr. Bott, let me introduce Dr. Hannah Green, who is something of an expert on the Neolithic in the western Mediterranean."

Bott took her proffered right hand in his left and held it at arm's length, as if inspecting the goods. He had large, calloused hands, more suitable to a laborer than a hotel keeper.

"Ollie, call me Ollie," he insisted in a rural accent that Hannah just couldn't place. "You've just gone and missed Aunt Alice. Well, never mind. She's not much for conversation, is she, Tuliver?" He paused for a few moments, smiling. "Now, now. So you're our expert, huh?"

What kind of bullshit had Tuliver been feeding this guy? Hannah dislodged her hand by turning her wrist against Bott's thumb and backed off a step.

"Well, I'm not exactly an authority . . . ," she began.

"Nonsense. Recognized those potsherds, didn't you?" Bott's tone was commanding; he'd paid for an expert and, damn it, he had better get one. There was a moment of tension.

"Now, now. I guess the young lady's just being modest. I appreciate that in a scholar . . . and a woman," he added.

Hannah couldn't tell whether Bott was evaluating her as an archaeologist or as a potential date, and she didn't much care for either. As for the "young lady" crack, well, she guessed that he was no more than five years her senior.

"This is a beautiful old home," she said graciously, "and you have such imaginative plans for it."

Bott smiled broadly, taking the irony as a display of interest.

"Indeed it is. My grandmother Eugenia built the place years ago. Story goes that she'd made a packet on the stock market and put most of it into this replica of the family home out in the west of England somewhere." He gestured widely and let his eyes wander over the dark-paneled room. "She was real fond of this place, Genie was. Turned it into a girls' school, she did."

"Her final resting place is actually on the island, I understand," Tuliver interjected, seeking a way to ingratiate himself back into the conversation. It was all very well for Green to create a good impression, but Bott's attention was as much his property as the data from the site.

Tuliver's query was ignored as if it were background noise.

"Now then," continued Ollie in a back-to-business tone. "So tell me, Doc, what do you make of our little old site. Impressed, were you?"

"Well, I'm certainly intrigued," she began cautiously. "But it's rather too early to say . . ."

"Too early?"

Bott's voice boomed out, and all conversations stopped. Only the baseball announcer's jabber and the distant thrum of what might have been a helicopter could be heard. Tuliver began dancing a nervous sidestep. But Hannah had never been one to back off from confrontation in archaeological matters, and she was unimpressed by petulant behavior, regardless of the status of the perpetrator.

". . . to say exactly what it represents or exactly who created it," she concluded, unperturbed. "I assume that's why Ian is keeping the project under wraps for now."

"Ah. Yes. Well," began Tuliver who was suddenly conscious of being the focus of every set of eyes in the room. "What Dr. Green means is that, ah . . . we can't be sure exactly what kind of social unit created the mound. Yes, the social unit. Band, tribe, chiefdom, that sort of thing. What do they say about this in relation to the European Neolithic, Hannah?" concluded Tuliver, effectively handing this slippery baton to his colleague.

"I'm sure that Mr. Bott—Ollie—doesn't want to hear a lecture on social structure," began Hannah, but the patron's glare suggested otherwise. "Oh, very well. But be warned: this one has sent plenty of students to the registrar's office to see if the 'drop' period is over." The joke fell flat, but Hannah soldiered on.

"First, you should know that years ago, social anthropologists noticed that human communities can be divided up into several types, based partly on how the group makes decisions or on who's in charge, if anyone."

"In my experience, Doc, there's always someone in charge," interjected Ollie Bott. Clearly, he was used to being that one.

"Yes, but some groups are more egalitarian than others. Look here."

She pulled a red marking pen out of her pocket and, resting on the back of the couch, began to draw a series of circles and arrows on a paper plate. Bott shuffled forward in his chair, craning his neck for a better view.

"Here, on the small population end are what we call **band** societies. People like the Australian Aborigines. They live in mobile groups of a few dozen and make their living by hunting and foraging."

Bott sniffed. "Didn't they used to be called **hunter-gatherers**? The men did the hunting, and the women did the gathering. I recognize politically correct language when I hear it, Doc."

Hannah wasn't going to get drawn into *that* argument.

"No," said she evenly. "If you think about it, foraging and gathering are really two different activities. *Gathering* implies going after vegetable foods, but *a forager* will take whatever's available. Like an animal that's already dead. Band societies move around a lot. They make temporary settlements wherever they go and follow the food resources. But they don't wander aimlessly. This month, they may be taking advantage of a fish run, and next they'll be harvesting seeds.

"From what social anthropologists tell us, their social organization is quite egalitarian. There's no individual that every member of the band looks up to as *the boss*. If there's a job to be done that needs skilled organization—like a fishing trip—the group chooses someone who is respected for that particular skill. But authority is quite fleeting. Running the show today doesn't give you command tomorrow. Anyway, using analogy based on these living groups, archaeologists have concluded that the earliest human communities—the folks who were around in the Paleolithic—all lived in bands."

Bott rubbed his chin thoughtfully and settled back into his chair.

"Sound like a bunch of pinkos to me. Don't reckon an outfit like that could organize itself to build my mound."

Hannah nodded, quietly pleased with her success in interesting Bott, who was probably more at home on the range than in academic discussions.

"I think a lot of archaeologists would agree with you there. At least with the organization part. Before people start building permanent architecture, we see them living in larger groups, say a few hundred or a thousand. I think that you'd be far more at home with these communities. Most are farmers or animal herders. Social anthropologists call them *tribes*, or **segmentary societies**. The Hopi are a modern example. Each Hopi pueblo is basically an autonomous town, and their societies are quite egalitarian. Although group decisions are made by clan elders, and every resident identifies him- or herself primarily by his or her pueblo and clan, all of them are also aware that they are part of a larger unit, the Hopi people."

"Now, now," began Bott, his eyes half closed in concentration. "That's more like it. The Hopi were quite the builders. Their ancestors, the *Hisatsenom*, built Mesa Verde, as I recall. Don't doubt that they could have put my mound up if they had a mind to."

Hannah lifted an eyebrow. *So, the rough, bluff Mr. Bott throws out the Hopi language name for the people called Anasazi as if it were a matter of common knowledge.* Perhaps her first impression was off the mark.

"I'm sure you're right. Segmentary societies can muster a lot of manpower when they want to by getting together with neighboring communi-

RUBBER BANDS AND STATES OF BLISS

or

 how one anthropologist classifies societies

BAND societies
☞ small mobile groups—egalitarian and kin-based
☞ hunter-foragers
☞ no permanent architecture
☞ e.g., modern Australian Aborigines and ancient Paleolithic peoples

SEGMENTARY societies
☞ groups of a few thousand—basically egalitarian but with cross-cutting social institutions
☞ farmers and herders
☞ permanent towns and religious structures
☞ e.g., modern Hopi of U.S. southwest and European peoples of the early Neolithic

CHIEFDOMS
☞ groups of several thousand ruled by hereditary leaders
☞ fortified towns, sophisticated subsistence system, and long-distance trade network
☞ large religious and defensive structures
☞ e.g., modern Indians of the U.S. northwest coast and prehistoric Mississippian culture

STATE societies
☞ highly populated cities with extensive infrastructure
☞ complex, bureaucratically-administered economic system supported by a standing army and judiciary
☞ very large religious and public buildings and religious structures
☞ e.g., modern Britain and dynastic Egypt

ties. In fact, the Neolithic people of western Europe who built mounds quite similar to yours are thought to have lived in segmentary societies. Even a small mound would have taken thousands of hours to build, which certainly suggests that people were working cooperatively."

"Quite so," said Tuliver, who was becoming annoyed with the way that Bott's attention was so fixed on his junior colleague. "By the time one gets up to the scale of a place like Stonehenge or Moundville in Alabama, we are talking hundreds of thousands of hours and even more centralized power. Wouldn't you say, Dr. Green?"

"That's right. People like the Native Americans here in Washington State and on the Northwest coast are quite centrally controlled. Anthropologists call them *ranked societies*, or **chiefdoms**, because, well, they are ruled by a chief. There's a lot of variation, but chiefdoms generally have populations between a couple of thousand and, say, twenty thousand. Their systems of agriculture are well organized enough to create a surplus of goods. And some of that goes to the chief as a tax. As far as the scale of mound building goes, the big difference between chiefdoms and segmentary societies is that the chief has the authority to organize and feed the hundreds, even thousands, of people working for months at a time that it would take to build a Stonehenge.

"Societies that are bigger than that tend to have a single ruler or a ruling elite. The people at the top are supported by a professional army that enforces the law and makes sure taxes get collected. It was pretty common for these state societies to have a class of priests, part of whose job was to warehouse agricultural surpluses. Some of the first bureaucrats were in the **state** societies of ancient Egypt, China, and Mesoamerica. It's only because they could collect, store, and redistribute vast amounts of resources that the early state societies could build stuff like the temples of **Tikal** in Guatemala, cities like Pakistan's **Mohenjo-Daro**, or the massive irrigation system constructed in Egypt during the New Kingdom."

Hannah threw her arms out to suggest the scale of these great engineering works and missed Tuliver's nose by an inch.

"But remember," she went on, "people lived in all these different types of societies at the same time in various parts of the world. The chiefdom that created Moundville was going strong about seven hundred years ago. While the final stage of Stonehenge was built by a society that was organized on similar lines about three thousand years earlier."

Bott nodded sagely.

"It's like a scale of evolution. At the low end, there's your band people, and at the high end there's people living in your state societies."

"No, no!" To Hannah, this was like lecturing freshmen. She just had to remember not to make it sound that way "It's not a question of *better* or *more developed*. These are just *different* types of societies. There's nothing intrinsically *better* about any of them. Humans aren't in a race to see who can develop the most complex social organization. Progress is strictly in the eye of the beholder, Ollie."

Bott put his head back and laughed.

"Now, now. This is quite the girl you have here, Tuliver." He paused, then turned to Hannah, the smile dropping from his face like a cloud crossing the sun. "But I ain't running no segmentary society here, and it's a risky business to tell the chief where he's wrong."

Hannah wasn't quite sure how to take this remark, but she was excused from considering it for too long as Alasdair arrived with a phone for Tuliver. He held his hand over the receiver and whispered, "It's Jean Grover in Seattle, from the International Geographic Society."

Tuliver snatched the instrument from Alasdair's hand with an impatient "yes, I know who Grover is," and turned to face the wall.

Big Dave ventured to suggest that Tuliver had let his subscription lapse, and Terry had to turn a laugh into a cough.

Even with a rear view, it was clear this was not a happy conversation. The back of Tuliver's bulging neck turned pink and then coronary red. He let out tiny spurts of air that didn't quite form words. Hannah wondered if he was having a seizure while Ollie Bott looked on blandly, as if Tuliver's discomfort were part of the floor show.

"Alasdair. Turn the television to the Seattle station immediately," said Tuliver coldly.

"Yeah, Al. I'm sick of that game, too," chimed in Big Dave, who seemed to have missed the point.

"I don't know which channel . . ." said Alasdair wretchedly.

"Will you find the bloody station!" yelled Tuliver, adding "useless twerp" as poor Alasdair clicked rapidly from one channel to the next.

Blazing with frustration, Tuliver snatched the remote control and in a couple of clicks settled on a newsroom scene. A perfectly coiffed man was speaking against a background of ax-wielding Vikings wearing horned helmets under a title that screamed, "Ancient Site Found on Dougal's Island."

". . . and now over to undercover investigative reporter Patty Patterson, reporting live from news copter 5."

Alasdair didn't hear what she had to say.

Just a glance at the face of his one-time lover Patty, and poor Alasdair crumpled into a heap on the floor.

CHAPTER SIX
"M" IS FOR MATERIALISM

In Which We Look into the Mind of a Cannibal

As if conjured by Tuliver's fury, a storm front blew into the Northwest overnight. Rain from the Canadian Aleutians pounded the brown shingles on the old school's roof. The wind moaned gothically through window frames and under doors.

While Hannah Green slept like the proverbial rock on her pile of blankets, the broken window in her private bathroom had not proven to be much of an impediment to the wind-driven rain. By morning the floor was awash, and the clothes she had worn the previous day lay like sodden rags. Worse still, her black going-to-meetings dress that she had so carefully hung from a nail in the wall was now saturated, having slurped up the rainwater like a sponge. Hannah closed the door. Even her powerful superego could not make a convincing case for dealing with this kind of mess at six in the morning.

The soggy scene far behind, Hannah ran more gingerly than usual across the damp forest floor. She really didn't want to repeat the slip and excruciating sprain she had endured on a rainy February morning out by the creek at Ennui State. Something like that was bound to make you careful, she told herself, but she wanted to run, really run, not just jog along like . . . like someone her age.

Turning away from the pine woods at the place where only the day before she had spotted the glint of binoculars, the runner made her way between high shrubs on a narrow path across the terrace that overlooked the ocean. The ground was sandy and drier here, and Hannah increased the rate of her pounding feet to somewhere between trot and canter. For a moment she thought she glimpsed a figure in a broad-brimmed hat out there on the edge of the woods. But before she could focus, it was gone. Must have been light on the trees.

She ran in the direction of the tower, whose crenellated top was occasionally visible to guide her above the bushes that fringed the path. The ocean sound was louder now. A muffled roar somewhere over to the left was occasionally punctuated by the crash of a breaker against the cliff face far below.

As the vegetation thinned, the tower came more or less into view. It was of gray stone and perhaps forty feet high. Austere and square, there wasn't much romance about the thing up close. Several adventurous plants had taken root in a crack that opened up from the corner of an upper window and stretched across the tower's face like a great scar. More likely to be someone's paranoid idea of World War II preparedness than anything else, thought Hannah.

Near the foot of the structure, she spotted a blob of unnatural shape and turquoise shade. She slowed to a walk. There was no mistaking that particular garment.

Alasdair Crisp was crouched on a rock, hunched over with his head in his hands. Seeing Hannah, he leaped to his feet as if he'd been stung. Hannah gave a wave and ran on, feeling she couldn't very well just turn around. Now she could see a nylon sheet sticking out like a low roof from one of the tower's walls, and the flicker of a campfire that had been obscured by the scrub. But more surprising still was the lanky form of Claude the Rock Man still in his sleeping bag, propped up on one elbow in his makeshift tent and sipping from a mug of something hot.

"Now look who's here," said the reclining one good-naturedly. He began to peel an orange with a knife that could have skewered a rhino. "It's my friend's mom from off'n that ol' ferryboat. Take a load off, ma'am. Coffee?"

Sean's "mom" trotted to a stop and pushed some escaping curls back under her headband. She grinned recognition at Alasdair, who nodded sheepishly in return with the look of a rabbi who'd been caught with a BLT.

"The young man here and me, we've been having a real nice talk about the Washington Indians," said he amicably.

"Really?" Alasdair's expression told Hannah that they had been discussing nothing of the sort.

"Cannibals they were," continued Claude. He shoved several orange segments into his mouth, and juice ran down his chin.

"Well, sort of," said Alasdair quietly, as if embarrassed by Claude's words. During his encounter with Tuliver on the previous evening, the young man had shown an inclination to bob from one foot to the other when excited or upset. Now, he was weaving like a boxer!

"Sick sons-of-bitches," stated Claude with finality. His tone indicated little concern with the ethnographic niceties of this practice. "Ain't no other way to explain it. So don't give me any of your 'cultural relativity' horseshit, Al. It gets up my nose the way you anthropologists try an' justify every sicko pre-version by saying that it's all relative."

It was impossible for Hannah to just listen. Rock Man obviously got his information from Rush Limbaugh. A century of anthropological scholarship notwithstanding, it was difficult to argue with such an authoritative source.

"Now just what kind of depravity have you been trying to explain away, Alasdair?" asked Hannah. Her tone was mockingly serious, and Claude's face cracked into a wide grin. He showed teeth that would have paid for an orthodontist's BMW as he turned to see how the young man would respond.

"Anyone would have to be a real idiot," went on Hannah after it was clear that Alasdair was not going to offer an opinion, "to think that **cultural relativity** makes every kind of behavior OK."

Claude nodded his approval and tore off another segment of his orange with his teeth.

"No. All relativity means to an anthropologist is that if you want to study or understand some aspect of another culture—such as cannibalism—you have to put aside your own feelings about it. Whether you personally approve of the practice or not. Or whether you'd do it yourself. That way you can gather information about the subject in a fairly objective way."

Rock Man was shaking his head.

"I know what you're going to say, Claude. That people *should* have opinions about whether something is right or wrong. And I think you're right. But just because I may sometimes disengage my personal ethics when I'm doing research, it doesn't mean that I don't reengage them when I'm done. An anthropologist could study violent street gangs or the subculture of drug users to find out why they exist and how their members came to be there. But she won't end up accepting either that gangs are a *good thing* for society or that heroin should be sold in Safeway. Of course, cultural relativity can be a dangerous attitude to bring to everyday life, except in the sense of 'live and let live.' But as a technique for research, it's pretty much essential."

"This is one persuasive little lady," acknowledged Claude with a nod in Alasdair's direction. "But seems to me that some things don't need no studying. Good old American common sense tells us what they're all about."

"Like cannibalism, for instance?" suggested Hannah. "Oddly enough, we anthropologists sometimes find it useful to put aside what you call 'common sense' because it's rooted in cultural assumptions. The view of the world that makes sense to the people we are studying—the **emic** view, we call it—is only one way to see things. The social scientist can also make up **etic** categories that describe situations in entirely different ways. For example, a person might have a variety of dinnerware in the kitchen cupboard, some of which is used everyday—the 'ordinary stuff'—and some only on special occasions, the 'fine china.' We'd call these emic categories. But through technological analysis, a researcher might discover that the two types are made of different ceramic types, have different glazes, and so on. The scientist's technical description, the etic analysis, lets her compare one household's idea of 'fine china' with the neighbor's. The scientific description might not make any sense at all to the people whose pots she's looking at. But by making up her own categories rather than using theirs, she has a basis for comparison."

"I guess so," said Claude reluctantly. "But what's there to know 'bout folks who chow down on other folks? They do it 'cause they don't know no better. Or 'cause they're starving."

"Sure, those are two possible explanations. But there are more, wouldn't you say, Alasdair?" Hannah looked hopefully over at the student, who had calmed considerably and was helping himself to coffee from Claude's enamel jug in a familiar sort of way.

"Naturally," he said, as if Hannah had made the most banal observation. "In my humble opinion, there are some very convincing arguments that explain that cannibalism was actually a response to ecological pressure."

PUTTING THINGS INTO CATEGORIES

Instead of conceiving of everything as **unique**, people categorize stuff by its most important **characteristics** according to what they want to **do** with the information.

Confronted with a large dog, the pizza delivery guy is likely to think of it as either **friendly** (won't bite) or **unfriendly** (may bite). But to a dog breeder the same animal is either **purebred** or a **mutt**.

Neither pair of categories is intrinsically better than the other. Each is **useful** in one context but not in the other. See what I mean?

The SCIENTIST classifies animals by their biological attributes: **mammals** have hair, **birds** grow feathers, and **fish** breathe with gills. Anthropologists call these ETIC categories, to denote distinctions that are made by the scientific observer.

THE SCIENTIST

Mammal

Bird

Fish

THE JEW

Yet, the traditional observant **JEW** sees the same beasts quite differently. Using rules derived from the Hebrew Bible and other religious sources, he divides them into *kosher* and *treyfe*—animals that may be eaten and those that may not. Distinctions like these, which are used by people in a specific social or cultural context, are called **EMIC** categories.

Treyfe (forbidden to eat)

Kosher (fitting to eat)

Again, Hannah locked her jaw to avoid sallying forth with a critique, and she braced herself against the materialism that she knew was certain to follow. To think that one could explain with such finality the *why* of any cultural practice was the kind of self-deception to which beginners were particularly inclined.

He'll start with the Aztecs, she thought.

"The **Aztec** civilization is a good example," began Alasdair confidently.

"Their agricultural economy was based on growing enormous quantities of maize to feed the huge population. They burned much of the land for agriculture, which took away the habitat of the wild game that provided the protein they needed. Unlike, say, the Asian civilizations, the Aztecs had virtually nothing in the way of domesticated animals. The end result was they had an unmet physiological need for protein and fats in their diet. And since there were more humans than strictly necessary to maintain a breeding population, they developed ritual cannibalism as a rational solution to the problem.

"They'd march a prisoner up to the top of the pyramid temple, slice open his chest, and pull out his beating heart before rolling the corpse down the side. Over twenty thousand were sacrificed at the Temple of Huitzilopochtli in 1487 alone," concluded Alasdair, as if describing how to make a taco.

"So they worked it all out, did they?" asked Claude, who didn't seem bothered by the R-rated description. "They needed the protein, so they'd eat their prisoners? And they made up a bunch of religious mumbo-jumbo to justify it to them who was getting ate up?"

Alasdair nodded, and the two seemed happy to leave it at that, when Hannah jumped into the discussion.

"Interesting. But it's only one way to look at cannibalism."

Turning to Claude, she said, "Alasdair gave what we call a *materialist* interpretation. What I mean is this: He's looked at the practice with the assumption that it *had* a purpose we can know, some goal to be achieved; and the goal was basically utilitarian—to fulfill some biological need. He sees Aztec society as an entity that made rational decisions to maintain its own existence."

"Like some big corporation laying off workers during slack times, to save money."

"You're right. In fact, that's one of the biggest criticisms of the materialist model. It assumes that everyone all over the world and at all times in the past has had the mentality of a modern Western businessman."

"But the model works," insisted Alasdair. "It shows a logical relationship between environmental conditions and people's response. Take the 1454 famine in the Valley of Mexico. Nearly half of the population is dying of starvation, and the Aztec priests insist it's because the gods are unhappy with the quantity of human sacrifice. More people are killed, and some of the pressure's taken off the food supply. You don't have to be a businessman to figure that one out."

"True," said Hannah. "But cannibalism and human sacrifice weren't devised to deal with the famine; they already existed. All the priests did was expand the practice. I'll grant you that reducing the population resulted in relatively more food, but you cannot say this is *why* the Aztecs did it. That's nothing but post hoc reasoning. Just because there's some outcome, you can't know that it was the *intention* of the participants: Wham! Bam! Cause and effect.

"Sure, there's a relationship between cannibalism and nutrition. But it would be naive to say that the participants planned it out or that they were aware of it at all. That's just **teleology**. Eating human flesh may have made some Aztecs healthier, and it may even have improved their ability to reproduce successfully (which in the long run, some would say, is the only important outcome). But is it right to say this is *why* they did it?"

Hannah looked from face to blank face.

"Well, damn it, why *did* they lunch on their people?" demanded Claude in frustration.

"That's my point. As far as the Aztec priests were concerned, they weren't eating lunch at all. They were saving the world. Catholics don't go to communion to take in calories, do they?"

Rock Man shrugged. "Damned if I know."

"If you asked an Aztec why he was sacrificing another human and eating part of his body, he'd have said he *had* to do it to keep the world in balance. If the rituals weren't performed, he'd say, the gods would cause all manner of pain and trouble for people. Sacrifice was a sacred event. Human flesh wasn't eaten like a fast-food lunch at a burger joint. Listen. When the Aztec priest was just about to kill the victim, he'd say, 'Here is my beloved son.' And the other would reply, 'Here is my beloved father.'

So, in a sense the priest was killing his own child. The same goes for the Kwakiutl groups here in Washington. Traditionally, they thought of all animals as humans in magical disguise. So when you eat salmon, you're eating a human being. You're a cannibal. To eat salmon is a sacred act to the Kwakiutl. It makes you a part of the great cycle of life and death."

She paused now and wiped away the beads of sweat that had developed on her forehead. Her legs were starting to cramp up. But Hannah's small audience was entirely still, eyes fixed on her expectantly, waiting for the last word.

"What this comes down to," she said, accepting an orange segment from Claude, "is that you can't ask *why* people carry out a certain ritual or cultural practice and expect a single cut-and-dried answer that you can put in a bottle on the shelf and label 'The One Truth.' Ask a materialist like Alasdair, and he's going to emphasize the social *effects* of carrying out the practice—an etic explanation. Ask a culturalist like me, and I'm going to give an emic answer and tell you what the ritual means to the people themselves. The two of us are coming from different perspectives, so naturally we emphasize different parts of reality. I'd be the last one to deny Alasdair's point that a society's adaptation to the physical conditions of life determines whether or not it survives. Of course that's right. But it's also true that human behavior is more than just a reflection of economic necessity, because *culture* determines *what* people perceive as reality. Their culture sits like a filter between the physical world and people's perception of it."

"Never thought of myself as Jell-O in a mold before," muttered Claude. "But see here, you've got two different ways of looking at this cannibalism thing. How d'you decide which is the better explanation, the mater'alist or the cult'ralist?"

Rock Man might not have had much in the way of a formal education, but he could follow a line of reasoning as well as anyone and wouldn't let go until he was satisfied that it made sense.

"To begin with, I wouldn't judge them by asking which one is right and which is wrong. And in this case there's no need to choose one over the other, since the explanations aren't contradictory. I'd rather think about whether or not they can give insights that are *useful* in helping me to understand this particular behavior."

Claude gave a long, head-thrown-back laugh and began to shuffle out

WHAT HE THOUGHT HE SAID...

"Marry me and we'll... live happily ever after!"

WHAT HE MAY HAVE MEANT...

*" Marry me and we'll . . .
reproduce the existing
system of gender roles!"*

*" Marry me and we'll . . .
maximize our contribution
to the gene pool!"*

*" Marry me and we'll . . .
improve our families'
social status!"*

WHAT DOES IT MEAN TO ASK "WHY?"

Ask someone **why** she is doing something and she'll probably tell you her **motivation**:

I'm hungry.
I'm in love.
I'm doing the right thing.

But when so many people are doing the same thing that it affects society as a whole, "why" is no longer only a question of **individual** motivation. That kind of highly patterned behavior has **outcomes** that affect power relations, social structure, ecological adaptation, and other aspects of society.

When this happens it's useful to see these behaviors as a way in which a culture makes things happen.

A theoretical model is a **lens** that we can look through to help us see culturally patterned behavior from some perspective. Each lens can give us a glimpse of one of the structures that is behind what we like to think of os individual choice.

Is the **outcome** the reason "why" things happen?

What does is **mean** to ask "why?

of his sleeping bag, chuckling to himself. As the bag unzipped, his guest was relieved to see that he was fully dressed. A damp waft of sweat confirmed that the jeans and T-shirt ensemble had been his night attire.

"Well now, that was quite a little talk. And I 'preciate you taking the time."

Hannah told him not to mention it. She was anxious to be off before her calf muscles seized up. And what was more, this little sidetrack had given her some ideas for "C Is for Cannibal." Perhaps she could come up with some gory pictures for a cover illustration. That would surely make her editor happy. For every publisher knows violence is a close runner-up to sex on the scale of academic audience appeal.

"And while you're here," continued Claude, ducking into his tent, "let me show you something real special. Seeing as you're so interested in ancient civilizations and all." The Rock Man emerged with a familiar green canvas bag, his hand grasping something wrapped in a wad of tissue paper. Alasdair groaned mournfully and covered his eyes, as if to will himself from the scene.

"Please Dad," he implored. "Not the goddamned Rocks o' Mystery again."

When Alasdair failed to show up at the site that morning, rumor and speculation proliferated like flies on . . . well, let's just say that there were a lot of them, and by ten o'clock there were as many theories as theorizers. The most popular scenario had Alasdair packing up his gear at midnight and taking the early ferry back to the mainland in disgrace.

Little Sandra Beech sighed sympathetically "It's, like, all over for poor Alasdair. Tuliver'll never let him finish his thesis now. How does that country song go? *An hour's fleshly pleasure brings a lifetime of regret.*'"

"Or ninety seconds' pleasure, in Alasdair's case," suggested Terry.

Sandra tittered.

In the absence of Alasdair, Terry had taken command and immediately sent the new guy off to rouse Tuliver and give him the bad news. Following the principle of "shoot the messenger," she thought it probable that the professor would be angry at Sean's report. But the kid was just a **digbum**, so there was little for him to fear from Tuliver. To the rest of them, Terry reflected, Tuliver was both employer and academic advisor—a position of double authority and peril.

Oblivious to his role in the dig's politics, Sean trotted back to the former school. There he found Tuliver and Ollie Bott together enjoying a leisurely breakfast of assorted pig parts, variously sliced, ground, and reassembled. Predictably, Tuliver was not happy with the news, but Bott's presence stopped him from haranguing the courier. He ordered Sean back to the site.

Tuliver made his entrance at 11:15, strolling up to the trench from which Hannah's nephew was lifting a couple of buckets of soil. Now, in Sean's defense it should be said that the buckets were unusually full and heavy, and that Tuliver appeared behind him without warning. The end result was that Sean overbalanced and stumbled into the trench, collapsing a section of its perfectly vertical side on his way down, and spilling his load back into the hole. Terry was about to call her assistant several variations of "dimwit" when she spotted a large, flat rock now exposed in the side of her excavation. While Tuliver fumed about the clumsiness of poorly trained excavators, Terry dropped to her knees and carefully troweled the soil from around the slab. Meanwhile, in his theatricals Tuliver had himself disregarded a basic rule of archaeological practice: don't stand too close to the side of the hole. A crack developed in the soil at his feet, and the professor jumped back to avoid joining the others in the trench. A huge block of soil sloughed into the excavation, knocking Terry backward and burying her legs in dark clay.

"Ohmygod, ohmygod," she squealed.

"Now don't panic, girl. You're all right," barked Tuliver, annoyed at what he took to be a melodramatic response to a simple accident.

"Of course I'm all right," Terry snapped back. "But just look at what's in the side of the frikkin' trench!"

The soil had slipped away from the edge of a large slab of rock, evidently the side of . . . something. Above and adjacent to it were wide, flat stones—walls and a roof under the unexcavated soil. Sean knew enough to back off, but Terry leaped to her feet and began to probe the void between the slabs while Tuliver climbed down into the trench.

"There's a space here," whispered Terry, "inside the rocks."

Breathing heavily, Tuliver elbowed his assistant aside and, with shaking hands, pulled a penlight from his pocket. It was dark inside the void, and the flashlight's battery was on the weak side, but it was strong enough.

"It's a cyst," he gasped. "A burial chamber. And . . . and . . . there are bones inside."

Then he sat back in the anarchy of disturbed soil and began to laugh, and Terry and Sean with him. They in the exhilaration of discovery, and he in the knowledge that Ian Tuliver, a minor academic from a midlevel university, had just found his ticket to the big time.

Tuliver's period of elation was brief. There were things to be done to secure his discovery. Brushing the dirt from the back of his trousers, the pudgy one gave orders to begin clearing away the loose soil and then almost skipped over to the site office and snatched the cellular phone from its cradle. Mr. Bott would be pleased!

Tuliver paused a few seconds, holding the phone, and considered the situation. This discovery had changed everything. Funding was no longer a problem. Institutions would be falling over each other to force money onto him. And although Bott was the landowner, he had become just another player. Things were about to change in their relationship, thought the archaeologist, expanding his chest with anticipation. It was he, Ian Tuliver, PhD, respected archaeologist and tenured professor of anthropology, who was calling the shots now.

Ten minutes later, Tuliver was back at the side of the trench, where Sean and Terry had been joined by the rest of the crew shoveling and bucketing soil. The atmosphere was lighthearted until Tuliver strode up barking out orders, looking dark and ill-tempered.

"Stop at once! All of you, back to your excavation units. And carry on with . . . whatever it was that you were doing. All of you," he added, looking straight at Dave the Neanderthal.

While the others drifted silently away and Tuliver turned back to the site office, Terry scrambled from the trench and leaped fearlessly in her boss's path, hands on hips, like the mother of a defiant teenager waiting for an explanation.

"Well?" she demanded.

Tuliver's anger flowed out of him like boiled-over milk.

Far from being excited or thankful, Bott had ordered him to close up the excavation unit and cover the burial cyst! Tuliver had reasoned and pleaded, but it was no good. Bott had even threatened to throw the entire crew off of the island if his orders weren't obeyed. Furthermore, to prevent any more unwanted visitors, Bott had phoned the ferry company early that morning and withdrawn permission for the ship to use his dock until Wednesday, so there was no way off the island. The situation was quite intolerable.

"Well, what does the moron want?" asked Terry, her voice picking up Tuliver's frustration.

"No one in the anthropology department is going to believe this," murmured Tuliver, more to himself than Terry. "He insists that we wait until the *International Geographic* team gets here on Wednesday. He wants us to open the cyst on camera!"

Lunchtime on the site was subdued. Tuliver's melancholy had turned the mood of the crew several shades grayer than at the moment of discovery. Terry had quite taken her professor's position and wailed about the unfairness of it all. Here was possibly the greatest find since—well, there wasn't anything to compare it with—and it was being manipulated by someone who wasn't even an archaeologist. The site was too important, she declared, to be the property of one person. Obviously, it should be taken over by the government and studied carefully over many years.

"The information in this site belongs to the people," expounded Terry. "It's part of everyone's history. At least, everyone in North America. It's not right that some moron can tell us how we should be doing our job just because he happens to own the land. No one can own the past," she said with passion, "it's not a commodity to be bought and sold. It's just too important.

"Information *wants* to be free. Think of the Internet. It's been a great force for egalitarianism and freedom just because no one controls it. Anyone can get a website and put up whatever she wants. The same goes for archaeology. We should be putting the information, our data, out there for everyone to look at from different perspectives. The alternative is a cabal of scholars—or so-called elders—hoarding the data so that no one can challenge their power. Take the Dead Sea Scrolls."

"OK, I'll take 'em," offered Big Dave, with a titter a full octave higher than one would have expected from him. Terry grimaced at him pityingly.

"The scrolls were kept secret for decades, and only a few people were allowed to see them, to study them. Well, it's the same thing here. Power and money are all that's important. The capitalists who have it get to decide what's right and wrong, to hold back scientific investigation, and to decide what the people get to hear."

Terry's monologue continued in much the same vein until she noticed that everyone except Big Dave had melted away back to work.

Tuliver was in the site office, so Terry sent Sean off to repair the ripped mesh on a shaker screen. She would spend the early afternoon writing up her field notes. Even if they weren't allowed to clean and excavate the cyst she could still take notes and do some photography, she supposed. Terry folded up the blue plastic tarp and sat in an empty wheelbarrow. Her notebook was open in front of her ready to receive her impressions of the morning, but the combination of rising early, a heavy lunch, and the pleasant coolness of the steel at her back brought on a drowsiness that soon turned to head-nodding and then to an out-and-out siesta.

As a rule, Terry avoided midday naps. They always seemed to end in frantic, paranoid dreams that left her feeling groggy and more tired than ever. This time she felt herself at the edge of a deep pit. The edge was collapsing, and she couldn't move her feet as the ground crumbled under her. Just as she began to slip away, there was a voice calling her name.

"Theresa! Are you ill, girl?"

Her eyes snapped open.

Dazed, she just managed to stop herself from overturning the wheelbarrow.

"No. Fine."

She grabbed her notebook from where it lay on the ground, stood up rapidly, and immediately wished that she hadn't, as a wave of queasiness welled up from inside. She fought it back.

"I'm fine. Just resting. Just taking a rest. Everything's fine."

"Will you kindly stop your babbling?" hissed Tuliver. "Had you been awake, you would know that everything is not fine. Far from it."

A group of half a dozen newcomers appeared behind Tuliver and a man stepped gingerly forward, overwhelming the professor with his size and antediluvian appearance. He was profoundly obese, and every movement seemed to give him distress. Sean noticed with surprise that two of the visitors carried rifles slung across their shoulders. He felt it safe to assume that (1) Tuliver had already spotted this particular feature, and (2) this was not the delegation from *International Geographic.*

The newcomer's snow-white hair was cut severely short, but his beard flowed over his chest. He motioned to one of his entourage, a redheaded young woman dressed like the rest in camouflage pants and shirt. She assembled a portable chair, into which he lowered his venerable mass. Sean gasped as he recognized Freya, and the two exchanged the briefest of smiles. He also recognized the large man's pained breathing as emphysema. It had been the same with his grandmother.

The bulky one's retinue gathered around, facing Tuliver as if to challenge him. However, the professor was resolved to stay in control of the situation. They were the interlopers. It was his site and his discovery. He had permission to be here. He was in charge. Tuliver puffed himself up and resolutely returned the leader's stare. In nearly twenty years of playing the game of academic politics, Tuliver had encountered egos of gargantuan magnitude and had generally been able to batter them down. The key was not to allow oneself to be impressed by the theatrical devices with which those egos surrounded themselves. Although, he noted, firearms were unusually effective in this regard.

"I am Magnus Gluteus, Priest of the Children of Odin," declared the large man as slowly as you would expect from one of his girth. "You have uncovered the bones of our ancestor." Tuliver found himself wondering where they found camouflage clothing to fit the gargantuan form.

"Now, I don't know what you've been told . . . ," began Tuliver.

The large one raised a hand.

"These are sacred remains and are not to be desecrated by your diggings and scrapings. They are not to be tested or groped over. They are for the ground."

He spoke with dignity and a level of solemnity that was disarming. Tuliver could deal with shouting—sarcasm and battles of words were his natural element. But sincerity was outside his comfort zone.

"This is a holy place dedicated to the ancestor who traveled here from Europe to settle this country so long ago. We, the Children of Odin, are his spiritual descendants. We are here to defend his bones." The large one turned to one of his supporters, a painfully thin man dressed like the rest in camouflage green, who eagerly stepped forward and announced that he was an attorney.

"The Children of Odin," he said with gravity, "will file a motion of habeas corpus. Unless you claim nolo contendere, we have the resources to respond by appealing to jus divinum. I warn you that ignorantia juris neminem excusat and that we intend to defend our pater patriae in saecula saeculorum!" The lawyer nodded gravely. He seemed to think that he had imparted some kind of information to the puzzled professor, who had no idea at all what had just been said.

Magnus returned the nod and began to speak. After every few words he paused to catch his breath. This added to the sense of anticipation as well as solemnity, for Tuliver expected the whale to keel over at any moment.

"We have not come to make trouble. We understand that you are seekers of the truth in your own way. But you must understand that what you propose is desecration. Our religion is ancient and our beliefs are to be respected. This we insist on. Why should it be that only the Christians and the descendants of Cain are given rights under the law? This we shall not accept.

"And this is not the first time the graves of our holy ancestors have been despoiled by archaeological diggings and their history misrepresented. The ancestor found not far from here was claimed by Indians, and yet your own archaeological tests have shown him to be a Caucasian."

As the large one paused to gasp in some air, Tuliver took up the subject.

"If you're talking about the nine-thousand-year-old skeleton called **Kennewick Man**, you've really got the wrong end of the stick. It's true that it lacks certain features common to American Indians and Asiatics—like spatulate incisors. But that doesn't prove he was a European. In every population you'll find individuals who don't have characteristics that are the statistical norm. Now, if archaeologists begin to discover an entire population that has distinctive traits, well then we would be able to give your, ah, theory some credibility."

As he warmed up, Tuliver's confidence began to blossom.

"As it is, there's no such evidence. And furthermore, what I propose to do on this site and with these remains is entirely between myself and the owner of the land, Mr. Bott. I shall excavate them in a scientific fashion, subject them to appropriate analyses, and publish the results. You and your troupe of refugees from an army surplus store will have no say in the matter."

Whether Magnus was breathing so deeply out of medical necessity or restrained anger was unclear. The volume and rate of his wheezing had increased during Tuliver's oration and was causing concern for his red-headed companion. The young woman placed a caring hand on his wide shoulder and whispered gently into his ear, while the armed men who flanked him fingered their rifles suggestively. The large one nodded and, with a deep sigh and a last glance at Tuliver, heaved himself to his feet.

Big Dave rubbed the stubble on his broad chin. "Fair-sized guy, that," he observed appreciatively.

After their visitors left, the archaeologists held an impromptu meeting. It was clear, said Tuliver, staring directly at Sean, that someone would have to stay and guard the site that night. Just exactly what that someone was expected to do if anything troublesome occurred wasn't so clear. Neither was Sean quite certain how he came to be honored with the job.

Having picked the lucky winner in that night's campout sweepstakes, Tuliver disappeared back to his office, leaving his crew puzzled and, in Terry's case, angry.

"See?" she demanded. "Here's another frikkin' bunch that thinks it has the right to tell archaeologists what they may or may not study. Here we are with an incredibly important scientific discovery that might just rewrite the history of North America, and we've got capitalists and pagans telling us how we should go about it. It's like I said. They just want to keep the information bottled up. Gaah!"

She concluded by kicking an innocent plastic bucket into the canvas side of the finds tent.

Sandra was swept away by Terry's rhetoric and wanted to say something intelligent and supportive, but she bit her lip instead. She was sure that Terry already thought she was an airhead. Why come out with something dumb and have her suspicion confirmed?

"Yeah, important to you. But some people have different values about that."

Terry turned and glared at Sean. She was not in the mood to be challenged by a mere digbum.

But the digbum continued.

"Some people—traditional native people, I mean—think that some information shouldn't be out there for everyone to see. And they don't care if scientists want to know."

"What *are* you talking about?" interrupted Terry in her tone of long-suffering.

"I guess I'm thinking of people like the Hopi clans down in the Southwest. There are some things each clan wants to keep to itself. Like sacred places on the landscape, stories, and rituals. Stuff like that."

"Religious mumbo jumbo," snorted Terry. "Archaeological sites contain important information. You can't have some group telling you what sites you can or cannot dig."

"Couldn't they just let us dig the ones that aren't sacred?" offered Sandra nervously. "Or do they not like archaeology at all?"

"A lot of Hopi think that archaeology is fine," said Sean, "because it gives them more information about their clan migrations and how they got to be on the mesas where they live now. Not that they need archaeology to confirm that. They already have oral histories and sacred stories. But some places are out of bounds. It might look like an ordinary archaeological site to you or me—only a bunch of pottery sherds and stone tools. But to some Hopi elder it's more than that. Perhaps it's the place where oral history says that two supernatural beings had a battle. Or where the Hopi Creator told them a story about their origins. So a site could be more important than just the information that we archaeologists can get out of it. And sometimes that information just shouldn't be out there for everyone to see."

"What about the Children of Odin?" asked Sandra. "Do they have a right to say whether we should be digging here? They have religious values, don't they?"

Terry harrumphed loudly, and Sandra knew that she should have kept quiet.

"I'm not sure about that," replied Sean seriously, to show everyone he thought Sandra had made a good point.

"I certainly wouldn't want to say that just because they're not qualified archaeologists they're plain wrong. It's like the Hopi case in some ways. They aren't scientists and aren't interested in how scientists do their work. The same information that we use to work out chronologies and subsistence practices, they use for religious purposes. There's no need to say 'we're right and they're wrong.' And besides, Indian tribes are treated as

sovereign nations under federal law, right? Congress has already made the decision for us. So it doesn't much matter what you or I think, or what any archaeologist thinks."

"If you say so. But that doesn't answer her question," goaded Terry. "Do you listen to the Children of Odin with the same attention that you give to some Hopi elder?"

Sean mused a few moments, thinking of his beautiful goddess.

"I s'pose that depends on which one of the Children is doing the talking."

That evening, Sean found himself pushing twigs into the campfire that he'd built to while away the period between dinner and bedtime. It was too dark to read, but the smoke had kept the mosquitoes and tiny flying bugs at bay. It was quite pleasant to be out there in the woods all alone, with the first of the evening stars just becoming visible. He lay back on his sleeping bag—for it was too warm to get inside—and he began to doze.

Sean could not have slept for too long. The setting sun still glowed over the woods when he sensed soft, fragrant hair on his cheek and the weight of an arm across his chest. It all seemed very natural somehow, and quite wonderful.

Without a word, he turned toward her.

"G" IS FOR GENDER

In Which Controversy Is En-gendered

It was with a sense of foreboding that Hannah began to stretch for her early morning run.

And who could blame her? On both of the previous two mornings she had encountered some kind of weird scenario. It was almost as if she were being manipulated into these bizarre situations by an all-powerful force. Shakespeare might have believed that we were all characters in a piece of cosmic fiction whose entrances and exits were scripted by a capricious author for an obscure purpose of his own, but Hannah Green knew with as much certainty as she knew anything that she alone was responsible for her decisions.

And today she felt like running.

She took off at her warm-up pace down the wooded path toward the site, with the intention of looking in on Sean. Although the poor kid was getting all the bum tasks on this project, he was taking it all in good spirits, and she was proud of him for that. Living and working closely together in less than salubrious conditions made field archaeologists clear on their priorities: knowledge of French poststructuralism be damned; "plays well with others" was probably the best recommendation a beginner could earn, after "great cook."

The great rock dominated the clearing while, at its foot, the untidy piles of soil lay like waste from the burrowings of insignificant creatures. Sean was sprawled face down on his sleeping bag by the cold remains of a small fire, as naked as nature had created him.

Taking a radical detour to the left, Hannah jogged over to the excavation trench, where she planned to make enough of a racket to wake her sleeping nephew. And this she did, but not for the intended reason. The excavation was a wreck. A huge, flat stone had been wrenched from the side of the trench and thrown roughly on the surface that Terry had so carefully cleaned of every stray particle of detritus. And the wheelbarrow in which the girl had sat to take notes the day before had been upended. Soil was strewn around, trampled by heavy boots whose impressions were preserved in the loose dirt. The looters had ripped the flagstone side from the burial cyst and removed the bony contents, except for a few slivers.

The bones known briefly as Tuliver Man had been heisted.

His aunt's squawk of dismay roused Sean enough to open an eye and squint in the direction of the sound. He saw Hannah look at the mess thoughtfully for a moment, then dash over to the finds tent. She scampered back and jumped lightly down into the trench. By this time Sean himself was hopping on one leg trying to pull on his jeans, which he found is surprisingly difficult to accomplish without the benefit of underwear. He hadn't the foggiest idea what was up. However, he realized with all the brainpower of one who had been awake for less than a minute that whatever was wrong, it wouldn't help to appear in a condition of total undress.

The stuff hit the fan at great speed and in prodigious quantities later that morning. And most ended up sticking to Sean.

His aunt stayed around long enough to deflect some of the flying flak, but ultimately there was no getting around the fact that the site had been looted on Sean's watch. She asked him how it could have happened. How could he have slept through the looting of the site? But he gave her only grunts and averted eyes. Regardless, his was the disgrace, and he was going to have to deal with the consequences. And besides, other responsibilities were calling Hannah irresistibly.

As late as ten thirty that morning, the elusive "G Is for Gender" existed only as a much doodled-on page of yellow lined paper. Although she was well prepared with humming computer, pages of notes, and the mental image of a depleted bank account, the muse of inspiration had fluttered off, and Hannah found herself staring at spots on the wall of her dressing room and junking unwanted e-mail messages. She told herself that the morning's discovery was putting her off, but she didn't really

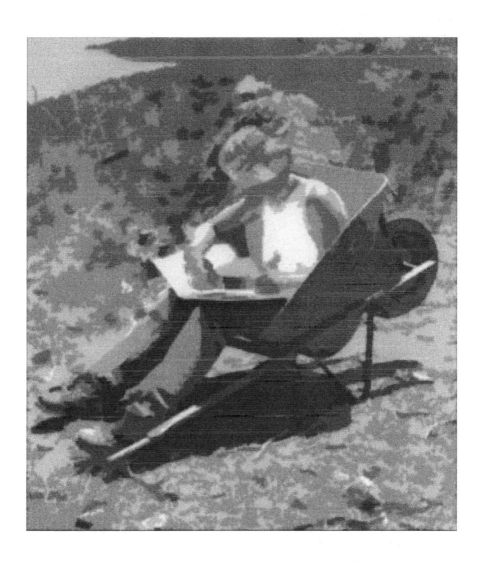

believe it. Normally, this was Hannah's most productive time of day, and she absolutely would not let it be wasted. The author packed up the laptop, stuffed her notes into a file folder, and headed for the great outdoors. Everyone was out wailing and moaning at the site, so it should be quiet enough.

Set up on the porch with a borrowed table and chair, a mug of strong tea, and a totally blank computer screen, Hannah was ready to start work. Again. And on the cusp of an entirely new set of distractions, the first of which was emerging from the woodland path in front of her.

Alasdair Crisp climbed sheepishly up the porch steps and offered Hannah a tentative smile. So different from the arrogant brat she had met just a few days earlier. For a moment, Hannah looked at the new arrival over the top of her glasses with an expectant expression. Then, to avoid an encore of his nervous dance, she motioned him to sit down.

Alasdair's preliminaries took a couple of minutes before he got to the point, which was to ask Hannah to intercede for him with Tuliver.

"How are the mighty fallen and the weapons of war perished," quoted Hannah silently.

She screwed up her face quizzically and turned a couple of bracelets on her tanned wrist. "This might not be the best time to approach him," she suggested. "Do you know about what happened last night?" The thought also passed through her mind that a recommendation from Hannah Green might be a condemnation in Tuliver s ears.

Alasdair had heard the news and insisted that, on the contrary, this was an especially auspicious moment to tackle the professor. For his own fault was nothing compared to Sean's mammoth screw-up.

He was temporarily humbled but still had work to do on his tact.

Reluctantly, Hannah agreed to the petition and for the second time that morning packed up her gear and stowed it in her bijou residence at the rear of the assembly hall. "G Is for Gender" was on hold yet again. Changing her shoes, she made her way back to the porch, where Alasdair was talking to a new arrival.

"The elderly lady in the hat said that Hannah Green is staying here," Hannah heard a familiar voice say.

"Yes. She'll be back in just a minute," replied Alasdair.

The response was three sneezes in rapid succession. Sneezes they were, but hardly recognizable as such. More like small, restrained explosions of air. It was surely how Queen Victoria would have done it, assuming she did it at all.

"Tshh! Tshh! Tshh! Damned allergies."

At the slam of the screen door, the stranger turned around, and she and Hannah grinned in mutual recognition.

bd starr was a good eight inches shorter than Hannah, although their weights may have been similar. Hanks of gray-streaked hair peeked out from under a hand-knitted beret of vaguely Scottish hues. The deep lines around her mouth and high furrows on her forehead showed that this was someone who offered more smiles than frowns. She and Hannah had been acquaintances since the Middle Ages back in undergraduate school when, before a brief marriage to her art history professor and a life-changing conversation with Germaine Greer in a Chicago elevator, bd had made her way through life as Bambi Denise Starzkopf. She and Hannah still hung out when they ran into each other at conferences.

Hannah didn't have to ask the reason for her friend's visit.

The Venus de 'Iuliver was right up her street, for bd starr was considered something of a rogue for her dedication to the field of ecofeminist archaeology. If she had not been awarded tenure in the Department of Art History at Somona State College because of her skilled teaching and tenacity, bd would surely have joined the bloated ranks of unemployed academics.

Typically, bd had not been put off by the lack of ferry service from the mainland. In spite of a profound inexperience in things nautical, she had charmed a dinghy out of Rick McDonald, set her pocket compass, and motored over to the island. Now she stood asking directions to the site from her old crony, Hannah Green. It was decided that the three should walk there together.

"Tshh! Tshh! Tshh! Damned allergies."

From the loose sleeve of her blue peasant blouse, bd took a used but carefully folded handkerchief and dabbed her nose. Not a tissue, you understand, but a real, off-white square of cotton embroidered with tiny red flowers and hemmed with a tiny, precise blanket stitch.

The two women spoke of this and that while Alasdair trailed behind, feeling out of sorts and even resentful toward the new arrival. Events of the last two days had brought Alasdair to the conclusion that Hannah

Green was worthy of his company, and he looked forward to discussing weighty matters of archaeological theory with her.

When the friends' conversation turned to the archaeology of **gender**, Alasdair let out a sound that was a cross between a splutter and a snort.

"I'm sorry," he said in a somewhat patronizing tone, "but in my humble opinion, sex and gender are really modern issues. The lives of people in the past, especially the deep past, were ruled by environmental considerations. Their biggest priority was to organize themselves in the most efficient way to eat and pass their genes on to the next generation. You only have to look at modern hunter-gatherers."

bd turned and cocked her head to one side.

"And of course that involved men going out bringin' home the bacon and women staying home with the babies, right, honey?" she offered innocently.

"Er, something like that."

Alasdair felt like he had just walked off the edge of a cliff. He wished that just for once he could keep his mouth shut.

"Matter of fact, honey," went on bd, "there's been a whole stack of ethnoarchaeological studies of the San people who live in the Kalahari Desert that found the opposite. Turns out that although hunting is a high-status, manly-man thing to do, women really bring in most of the food. In spite of having to take care of the children. But if we're going to talk about gender," continued bd, dropping back to walk beside him, "let's start by clarifying some concepts, OK?"

Alasdair nodded without much enthusiasm.

"First, there's sex. Biological sex. Male and female, defined by the primary and secondary sexual characteristics. Do I have to go into the details, honey?"

Alasdair felt himself blush horribly. He looked down at the path and watched the forest floor pass under his feet.

"Then there's gender. These are culturally constructed categories. Every society uses them to decide what's appropriate behavior for each gender. By and large, in American society males don't wear dresses, right, hon? And until recently, the only role for a *respectable* woman was wife and mother. And yet there's nothing intrinsically feminine about a dress or earrings, doing the washing, or working in an archaeological lab. It's just *our* cultural practice to associate these things with females."

A PALEOLITHIC FANTASY
[or Projecting 1950s Gender Roles into the Past]

→ He makes useful things out of rocks and lugs
dead animals home for dinner.
He's MAN THE HUNTER.

→ She gathers the occasional herb and stands
around looking decorative.
She's WOMAN THE DOMESTIC.

"Sure," granted Alasdair, as if stating the obvious. "There are two biological sexes and two corresponding genders."

"Oh really? Ever been to San Francisco?"

Alasdair smirked, but bd was speaking with an ethnographer's seriousness.

"How many gender variations could you count in the Castro District? Men who identify as women, women who live as men, and any other variable that you can think of—and probably some that you can't. There are lots of people whose gender doesn't conform with their sex, as far as mainstream American culture is concerned. And this isn't just a modern, underground phenomenon, in case that's what you were thinking. There are many traditional societies where the people recognize three, even four genders as easily and naturally as modern North Americans do two!"

"OK, but I don't suppose that's something archaeologists can deal with," shrugged Alasdair. bd wagged her head to imply maybe, maybe not.

"Without some kind of ethnographic text, it would be hard. The Chumash people of the southern California coast, for example, had a third gender called *aqi*: they were men who took on some of the gender roles of women, as well as being the group's undertakers. There's an archaeologist friend of mine, Sandy Hollimon, who thinks that she can identify these individuals by the female-associated artifacts that were buried with them.

"Ethnographers find in every culture that social roles, division of labor, and structures of power are closely related to gender. To a large extent, socializing kids is a matter of teaching them the culturally approved roles for their gender. Girls should act in this way. Wear these kinds of clothes. Model their behavior after adults of the same gender. And the same goes for little boys. It prepares them for the roles they'll play when they grow up and become functioning adults. Right, honey?"

Alasdair shrugged. bd reminded him of his mother.

"What's so bad about that?" he said. "Without some generally accepted norms you couldn't have organized society."

"Sure. No argument with that, hon. Problem is when our ideas about gender roles—which are culturally variable—get confounded with biological sex, which, by and large, is set at conception. End result is biological determinism: Women and men do what they do in society because of their sex. Gender roles come to be seen as 'natural' outcomes of our biological differences. And that leaves half the population . . ."

". . . pregnant, barefoot, and at the cooking hearth," said Hannah.

Alasdair gave a harrumph.

"Now you're talking politics, not archaeology." His companions would have jumped in there and then, but he went on rapidly. "What you say's all very well, but what does it have to do with archaeology?"

"That takes us to the **feminist** critique of archaeology," began bd. "Archaeologists have projected the male-headed household back into the ancient past. They wrote about women as dependent creatures who were anchored to their wifely duties around the home because of their children. On the other hand, men are seen as independent, coming and going as they wanted, and making all the important decisions by virtue of the fact that they supposedly supplied the food. A lot of archaeologists just assume that artifact types like stone hunting tools are things used by men. Pottery and textiles—the home crafts—supposedly represent women's work.

"And here's my point (and don't think I don't see you rolling your eyes, hon). When scientists make statements, they give them authority. People believe the guy in the white lab coat and think to themselves, 'It must be true because otherwise the Expert wouldn't be saying it.'

"So, when some paleoanthropologist comes up with a model of proto-human behavior that has mother Lucy staying home with the kids while daddy goes off hunting game, he makes it seem that these gender roles are actually biologically based. As if it's been that way among humans since before we were human. That it's right and natural that men's and women's roles should be as he says they used to be."

"Yeah, it's like I said," said Alasdair. "That's politics. Isn't there a way of bringing women into prehistory without"—he wanted to choose his words carefully here—"making a feminist statement? Can't you have an archaeology of gender that isn't so much like a political agenda?"

"Sure, hon. That's been done. But I'm rather cynical on the subject. If you don't go into archaeological interpretation thinking like a feminist, you reproduce all the old assumptions. Throw in a few references to female contributions and then go on with whatever you wanted to say in the first place. We call it the 'add women and stir' approach."

Alasdair shook his head.

"Sorry. I'm just not convinced. The feminist critique thing I get. It sounds reasonable, and I'm sure archaeologists will learn from it. But it's only that—a critique. It's not a theory. Not an explanatory framework or model like cultural materialism or human ecology. It gets you somewhere in terms of contemporary politics, civil rights, and all that sort of thing. It doesn't *explain* cultural change the way the great anthropological models do."

"That's a good insight, hon," said bd, resting her hand briefly on Alasdair's shoulder. "And in a sense you're right. But you've brought up the question of what the goals of archaeology should be. Can be. Those kinds of explanatory models work at an entirely different scale than what we've been talking about. The ecological anthropologists and others of the **processual** school are interested in seeing how history works itself out at the largest scale. How did the society go about managing its resources? How successful was it in the long run? But gender relations are played out on the small stage, in households and families. The two approaches can have quite different goals. Often they just pass each other by and don't stop to say hello. But I'm not saying a feminist archaeology of gender can't work on that scale. Just that it doesn't have to. Even when women work primarily in the household, their work is important for society at large."

The group paused for a few moments while bd balanced herself using Hannah's shoulder and pulled a twig from her sandal.

"Do you know Christine Hastorf's work on Inca society?" she went on, flicking the offending woody fragment into the air. "Women were responsible for making corn beer, a very important commodity that was central in the symbolic expression of Inca politics and power relations. By looking at seed remains as well as collagen from human bone, Hastorf concluded that although they took on more and more responsibility for making the beer, the women didn't get to drink it. So it seems clear that women's status declined through time from the pre-Inca period.

"And since we're talking about women south of the border, how about Elizabeth Brumfiel? She looked at society in the Valley of Mexico before and after the Aztec conquest. Women were responsible for weaving and cooking. Pretty dull, huh? Well, it turns out that the cloth they made, like Inca beer, wasn't just a utilitarian product. It was used like currency. Money. When the Aztecs came in, Brumfiel says, the valley cloth wasn't needed much anymore. People got it by exchange from other places in the Aztec empire. So women's labor was redirected toward making foods, like tortillas and dried foods. This says something about women's role in creating the mobile labor force that was so important to the Aztec economy.

"Even though changes in gender roles and gender-linked behavior are played out on the domestic stage, they can have great consequences. Is it worthwhile studying these changes, hon? And how they transformed people's lives? I'd say yes. But, from everything I've heard, you don't have to look any further than right here for a potential example of feminist archaeology."

She gestured toward the clearing up ahead, with its archaeological paraphernalia and bent-over workers, and the great rock overlooking them all.

"I'm not sure just what you mean," replied Alasdair, becoming more than a little sweaty this close to his destination, "but if it has anything to do with feminist archaeology, I don't suppose that Dr. Tuliver would agree."

From his vantage point behind the fallen pine tree, Sean could see it all and rather wished he couldn't. It was some kind of ritual—of that he was quite sure—with a lot of hands held aloft, a rather puny set of deer antlers, and a constant rhythmic chant.

"O-din. O-din. O-din. Hear our call!"

Once, a participant made a wrong turn in the group's circuit around the pyre that was the focus of their activity, and all the group members bumped into each other, one after the next. Like a crew of white-robed Keystone Kops. Perhaps Sean should leave? He didn't feel right about spying on the Children of Odin, but he'd come to get some answers and to redeem himself in the eyes of the other diggers.

It had been an ugly scene back at the site. Tuliver had all but accused him of stealing the burial himself. Or, at the very least, plotting to do it. Freya's momentary display of recognition the afternoon before had been captured by Tuliver's discerning eye, and Sean was forced to admit she had returned that evening. But his stubborn refusal to divulge any additional details of their encounter caused Tuliver's anger to boil into a seething mess of accusations and insults.

How had the camouflaged lunatics found out about the burial so quickly unless someone had told them? Sean had no idea.

How could they possibly have skulked onto the site and dug out the remains without being noticed?

Sean knew only too well but said nothing, as any gentleman would. He crept away confused and hurt, with Tuliver's shouts assailing his back like stinging flies.

The pine branch that had been sticking into his knee for the previous five minutes was finally enough of an annoyance for Sean to reposition himself behind the fallen tree. He was far enough from the celebrants to be unconcerned about his rustling and crackling sounds, which would surely be drowned out by the continued chant.

"O-din. O-din. O-din. Hear our call!"

Sean stifled a snorting laugh. This must be why religions had ritual languages—Latin, Hebrew, Sanskrit, and the rest—so the banality of what was being said wouldn't occur to the participants and make them collapse into a fit of the giggles. That would spoil the effect completely.

There was another pileup over at the ritual. The intoning voices stopped raggedly, and someone, possibly the Latin-spouting lawyer, was shouting in anger. Instinctively, Sean ducked his head behind the trunk of the great tree.

"Left. Right. What the hell does it matter *which* way I go?"

A white gown hit the ground, and a figure stomped off. "I'm outta here," he yelled over his shoulder. The five remaining Children were motionless for a few seconds, as if deciding what to do. There was some low mumbling, and four of the robes trouped off in a group.

Freya pulled back her hood and dejectedly watched them go. She looked around where the horns, the robe, and other accoutrements of the abandoned rite lay forlorn, then stooped to gather them up. It was a very melancholy scene, and it caused all Sean's anger to dissolve and his self-pity to evaporate like mist in the Washington morning. Explanations could wait. He just wanted to be with her, to comfort her.

"Oh my gawd, it's the lunatic fringe."

Tuliver shook his head in a give-me-strength sort of way and leaned dangerously far back on his chair. There was barely room in the trailer for all four, and his visitors clustered by the door. They were not invited inside. In his mind, Tuliver had good reason to detest them all for their respective contributions to his mounting frustrations: Alasdair Crisp, the turncoat; Hannah Green, a flirt whose idiot nephew had single-handedly destroyed the site; and that ridiculous bd starr, who set serious archaeology back twenty years with her absurd goddess prattle. What a noxious little band of reptiles they were.

"Good morning, Ian, honey. Aren't you going to invite us in?" said bd.

"Come in and sit down. Do."

Alasdair took the one chair, having never been taught to do otherwise. Then followed a silence that Tuliver refused to break. He leaned back even farther and folded his arms, looking expectantly at bd with his usual inscrutable smile.

"Know what I'm doing here?" asked bd.

Tuliver shrugged. "Can't imagine. Are you, perhaps, changing your area of interest from fiction to archaeology?"

That bd returned the smile, Tuliver found unsettling. It was as if she had a bombshell to drop on him and didn't mind stretching out the time before it was delivered, enjoying the anticipation.

"Oh, Ian, honey, you're such a humorist. Fact is, I was working over at the radiocarbon dating lab in Seattle and staying with Jean Grover . . ."Ah ha! He'd always suspected some kind of unnatural relationship there! "And since I had a day to spare she asked me to check out the site. Before the *Geographic* crew arrives, y'see."

The sugary smirk on Tuliver's face crumbled like meringue in the rain.

"She's interested in emphasizing the goddess component," continued bd, savoring the moment. "Thinks that the readership'll like that."

At this latest revelation, Tuliver turned ghostlike and had to grab the table to stop himself from losing balance.

"This is a joke, isn't it?" demanded Tuliver when he had recovered. "You're saying this to annoy. It's malicious and . . . and . . . and unprofessional," he concluded feebly.

bd shook her head gravely. "You know that's not true, Ian. Don't mean to come in and dictate to you, but Jean said to get the story straight. Before tomorrow."

"Story? What story? This is archaeology!" Tuliver threw his arms out wide as if to encompass the profusion of books, rolled maps, and other paraphernalia of Science-in-Action that filled the office. "The only *stories* here are those fairy goddess tales born of *your* imagination."

He thumped the table with a pudgy fist. A yellow mechanical pencil dropped to the floor and bounced directly into the waste bin. Although it was a thousand-to-one event, it was of no consequence.

Hannah put a calming hand on bd's shoulder. She could feel that her old friend was about to blow a vein as big and juicy as the one that now throbbed in Tuliver's bulgy neck.

"And you, Crisp," he barked, "had best get back to work. I'm not paying your expenses to sit around." Alasdair jumped up at the sound of his name and scuttled toward the door. "We shall speak later, young man," added Tuliver in a headmasterly tone.

Hannah straightened up to let Alasdair pass and decided to use the opportunity to duck out. "Sure you don't need me here, so I'll leave you two to your business." She followed the young man out the door. "Anyway, I've an errand to take care of."

Now that they were alone, bd pulled up the vacant chair so it faced Tuliver with only a box of papers on the floor between them. She sat primly, hands folded in front of her, and was about to make an opening move when she exploded into a festival of nasal dissonance.

"Tshh! Tshh! Tshh! Damned allergies."

Out came the handkerchief, and the sufferer patted the underside of her nose, which was feeling red and tender.

Tuliver sat unmoved, expressionless.

"Now, Ian, honey," began bd. "This is awkward for both of us. Hope that you believe me when I say I'm not here to usurp your position. Jean just wants to bring in another perspective."

"A woman's perspective, I suppose you mean." Tuliver turned, looked through the pitted screen of his office window, and continued in a flat tone. "I suppose the opinion of an experienced archaeologist who has paid his dues in the trenches no longer counts for anything."

She might have pointed out that Tuliver's experience "in the trenches" had been quite brief and many years before, but bd would take the high road. Or at least the middle road. She would appeal to his vanity. And lie a little.

"Not true, honey. Jean respects your work immensely And your commitment to scholarly cooperation. She quoted your own opinions about—

how does it go?—scholarly journals not being committed to 'enshrining some eternal Truth' but being open to other interpretations. Isn't that how it went?"

Tuliver pursed his lips but showed no sign of annoyance. At the time, he'd felt that it was a damned stupid thing to have said in public, an off-handed piece of inanity that had been snagged by the editor of the Society for American Archeology's newsletter. But the quote had earned him minor notoriety, and he was willing to own it.

"Yes, something like that. As you know," he continued, becoming expansive in the anticipation of expounding his own views, "I've never been of the opinion that one should restrain hypotheses simply because they have not yet received the imprimatur of the archaeological establishment. Academe should value diversity. Museums should be places of discourse, not shrines where the interpretations of the past are unchallenged through the generations."

"So you agree with authors who give their books names like *An Archaeology of Early American Life*, which a few years ago would have been *The Archaeology* . . . ?"

"Of course," he insisted with a wave of the hand. "The implication is that the author does not have the final word on the subject, and the data may be interpreted differently by someone else. Discussion and change are the bases of science, even social science."

To be strictly accurate, Tuliver was willing to spout these liberal ideas and even to believe them in a general sort of way. Except, of course, when it came to his own work.

"Exactly," said bd with a broad smile. "That's just what Jean was saying to the editor of *American Archeologist*. 'Ian Tuliver will put Stanford to shame,' she said."

"She said what?" Tuliver was puzzled, but intrigued.

"Oh, they were talking about how Stanford was putting all their data on the Web. From their excavations at **Çatalhöyük**, that is. And how you were likely to do the same." Tuliver's eyebrows rose slightly, causing bd to add, "since you are into online publishing."

Another slight exaggeration on her part.

Earlier that year, Tuliver had browbeaten a new graduate student into posting one of the professor's old publications, recycled from his doctoral

CATAL HOYUK
A Site... with a Website

CATAL HOYUK is a really nifty 7-8000 year-old Neolithic town site in Turkey. The site is made up of many buildings that were entered through holes in the roof. While many archaeologists guard their data until they publish, the **CATAL** **HOYUK** website gives access to excavators' field notes so anyone with a computer and an Internet connection can download, muse over, and reinterprete the data. The website also features an open discussion forum. Cool, eh?

dissertation, on the department's Web page, in the hope that it would get his name cited by Web-crawling researchers.

Turning back to the window, Tuliver considered the implications for a few moments. Çatalhöyük was one of the best-known research excavations in the world. A spectacular 8,000-year-old Neolithic town site in Turkey, first worked on during the 1960s and now a joint effort of scholars from Stanford, Berkeley, and prestigious institutions from around the world. Tuliver didn't mind being mentioned in the same sentence as that team. No objection at all. The Çatalhöyük website was famous for providing access to all the excavation data. While some hoarded their information until publication at some time in the nonspecific future, the Çatal project director, **Ian Hodder**, put it out there for anyone with a computer.

"Quite right. I was e-mailing just that to Hodder only the other day." The famous name dropped almost imperceptibly from his lips.

"Exactly," smiled bd, circling for the kill. "And that was where Jean saw the feminist connection, too."

"The *goddess* connection, you mean." His defenses were up again.

"If you want to put it that way. But remember, Hodder has a section on the Çatal Web page devoted to his discussions with the Goddess movement. And they tour the site, too."

"I knew that," Tuliver said curtly

His mind was moving rapidly, assessing the relative gain to be made by embracing this fringe group and thereby aligning himself with the postmodern aristocracy, versus the condemnation of the more conservative group whose banner he habitually flew.

"But just explain to me, if you'd be so good," he continued, "what Hodder has gained by engaging with these . . . these hairy-legged Wiccans?"

Although her allergies had abated, bd drew the handkerchief from her sleeve and delicately blotted her nose to the count of ten. If she could bear Tuliver's insolence for just a little longer . . .

"I'm sure you remember that James Mellaart, the first excavator of Çatal, found that many of its rooms were decorated with elaborate relief sculptures and paintings. He also found a lot of small figurines. And many of these have female characteristics, such as the so-called Mother Goddess figure. He took all this to mean that the Neolithic people who lived there had a female-centered religion. That the buildings he had dug up were their shrines."

Tuliver sniffed, though not from an allergic reaction.

"Which is why," he sneered, "the Goddess Gang thinks Çatal was the origin of what Gimbutus called 'Old Europe'—that mythical period of peaceful, egalitarian, matriarchal power that preceded the warlike empires of Greece and Rome. Yes, yes. We all know about that. But kindly explain what this mumbo jumbo has to do with the new interpretation of Çatal?"

"Quite simply, Mellaart was thinking like a modern Western man when he took the decorated buildings as having specialized, ritual functions. Unconsciously, he was looking to separate religious ritual—which he thought of as formal, hierarchical, and specialized, as it is in Western cultures—from the domestic sphere. The home, which women traditionally control.

"A feminist archaeologist like Hodder starts with a different postulate: Many so-called primitive peoples don't separate religious ritual and day-to-day family life. So during the Neolithic, the two were likely to have been, ah . . . inseparable. And recent excavations at Çatal suggest just that. Portions of the floors of the supposed 'shrines' contain ordinary domestic refuse. Other areas seem to be clean. So the same room may have had both household and ritual functions."

"Or it may not have," added Tuliver.

"And look at the figurines that some people think are female deities," continued bd. "Where are they found? Not in burials or ritual places. But in house walls, on floors, and in a home grain storage bin. The evidence is mounting that the home was the center of Çatal families' religious life—not some priest-dominated temple. Emphasizing women's roles, it's a feminist interpretation. And you don't have to be a follower of any goddess to see the value in it."

Tuliver placed his fingertips together in a small pyramid that he positioned under his chin, and closed his eyes. Was he being contemplative, or was he just ready for a nap? bd wondered.

"Well, that seems quite, ah . . . plausible," he went on cautiously. "And it is, one supposes, no different from any other politically motivated archaeological interpretation."

bd wasn't sure how to take this remark. She raised her chin questioningly.

"Surely you follow?" said he. "Your feminist approach is like Marxist archaeology in that both are interested in constructing a scientifically corroborated past that conforms to their political goals. They point out, quite correctly, that there is no such thing as 'raw data' in archaeology. The mere fact that we record some pieces of information and discard others is determined by our orientation going into the research. Just as archaeologists don't interpret their sites in an intellectual vacuum, neither do they work in a political void. Evidence our conversation this afternoon."

He fixed her with a particularly intense look that may have been equal parts thoughtful reflection and smirk, then turned to the window.

"I wonder," he continued wistfully, "what will become of the archaeologist's authority to interpret his—or her—site. If, in this postmodern world, all interpretations of archaeological discoveries are given a place at the table, why cannot just *anyone* dig and publish and be taken as seriously as the most respected professional? Is the profession of archaeologist worth anything if the opinion of some flowers-in-the-hair goddess seeker is equal to mine? When we discard the lifeline of objective science, where can we find ourselves but adrift in a sea of uncertainty?"

These questions did not seem to demand a response.

"Well, honey," said bd after a long silence. "Can't wait to see your site, though I must be out of here soon. I s'pose you'll want to start getting everything ready."

"Ready? Ready for what?"

Tuliver roused himself from his woolgathering and turned toward her.

"Why, for the *Geographic* crew, of course. Didn't I mention they were coming?"

"Yes, yes. But I'm sure they won't be about their business until tomorrow. To get the best light." Tuliver sounded confident in his assumption.

bd stood up, shaking her head.

"Oh no, hon. Quite the contrary. They want to set up lights and shoot tonight after dark. I imagine that they're going for a dramatic effect."

"Tonight?" bellowed Tuliver, leaping from his chair. "Tonight?"

bd grinned helplessly.

"Sorry, Ian. I'm just the messenger. Now, if you don't mind, I'll take a look around and then head back to the mainland."

With a shrug of the shoulders and one last dab at her nose, bd began to back out of the door. She found her way blocked by Hannah who, glancing up at an extremely agitated Tuliver, whispered something in the woman's ear and gestured toward a uniformed figure who began to walk toward the office.

"Looks like you-all have a visitor," said bd.

"Are the *Geographic* people here already?" he whined.

"Nope. It's a deputy sheriff. She's come to inspect the famous remains."

Tuliver's body jerked as if jolted by an electrical shook.

"Does everybody in the entire state of Washington know about this skeleton?"

Then his shoulders drooped, and his head fell in resignation.

bd felt something like compassion for the man and was on the verge of offering a word of sympathy when Tuliver regained control, evidenced by an adjustment of his tie, and abruptly announced, "All right. Wheel the witch in."

Her commiseration dispersed instantaneously, and bd left with neither word nor glance. Taking Hannah's arm, she hustled her toward the excavations, hoping that the deputy, a stone-faced woman with hair drawn back in a tight bun, would give him hell.

The casual spectator might have seen these two women move around the site with a quantity of sage head-shaking and lip-pursing. First to the finds tent, and then over to the excavation. But only the most observant would have noticed a small package that slipped between the two, which the shorter figure tucked safely into her sleeve next to the embroidered handkerchief.

"M" IS FOR MARX (KARL, THAT IS)

In Which Mr. Doyle's Ancestors Are Outed

D r. Ian Nigel Tuliver turned the lock on the office trailer door and slumped down into his chair.

What a day it had been!

First there had been the insane bd starr woman. Then that tight-lipped witch of a sheriff who, in her sly tone, had virtually accused Tuliver himself of making off with the skeleton. It was clear to him why cops wore those reflecting sunglasses. He would write a strongly worded note on university letterhead to her superior, that's what he would do.

The whole day had been exhausting. And there was still the *Geographic* crew to look forward to. Tuliver cradled his head in his hands and massaged his temples to clear a growing headache. Malicious colleagues, unappreciative superiors, overbearing sponsors, police harassment. The world certainly made it tough for an honest scholar these days.

On instruction, Alasdair had made sure the crew left early that afternoon. They were told to be back later to serve as human props for the photography session that evening. For much of the afternoon his chief had been entirely distracted by the sheriff. Then he had locked himself in the site office, yelling the occasional order through the window. So by default Alasdair was leader again, sucked back into his old role by the temporary vacuum of power and in spite of Terry's declaration that the site should be liberated and run as a cooperative.

The *Geographic* location crew—**Hans Wurst** the photographer, two lighting techs, and a sad-faced driver—arrived on the six o'clock ferry in a spotless SUV. The truck was so huge that anyone might wonder how the maker expected the thing to negotiate the narrow trails for which it was said to be designed. They used a cell phone to get directions, and by six thirty the beast had rolled onto the archaeological site with the sun still high enough to set up the portable generator and lights.

Either in a subtle homage to the late Danny Kaye or as a blatant rip-off of the same, the photographer's business card proclaimed himself "King of Photographers and Photographer of Kings." Tall and lanky with a shock of gray hair, Hans Wurst was dressed all in khaki, topped-off with a multipocketed vest that bulged with the arcane paraphernalia of the photographer's craft.

Like a cop at a crime scene, Hans commandeered the site, ordering lights and equipment arranged and rearranged as Alasdair, Terry, and Sandra sat on folding chairs drinking coffee and watching the unrolling of huge coils of orange electrical cord and the rigging of banks of silver-colored lights. While Big Dave good-naturedly volunteered to install the portable generator on a large stump behind the finds tent, Tuliver had not deigned to show up for these mere preliminaries. Like the main attraction he felt himself to be, the professor intended to appear just in time for the photography itself and to leave immediately thereafter.

Terry was sick both of being a spectator and of Alasdair's snide comments about the slow and inefficient manner of the photographer's helpers. And Sandra wasn't any better company, she thought grumpily. The blonde bimbo was inoffensive enough, but she doubted that the girl had an original idea in her head. Terry wandered over to the photographer's truck. Better a few honest words with a member of the working class than listening to Alasdair's reactionary drivel.

The long-faced young man's job was to drive, maintain the supplies, and schlep the heavier pieces of equipment. That was done now, and he had been sitting on the vehicle's massive rear bumper, swinging his legs and looking bored, when she approached him. Manuel—who pronounced his name as if describing a type of car transmission—was that most pitiful of workers, the student intern. Attracted by the romance of photography and the necessity of moving out of the dorm, the UCLA junior was spending his precious summer doing almost exactly the same things as if he'd been working for his Uncle Jaime's restaurant supply business.

"Only that would have been for pay," he said resentfully, prying a line of dirt from under his thumbnail with a sliver of wood. "Although this

116

job's a lot of fun sometimes. You gotta have a sense of humor when you ride with Hans Wurst," he added with the hint of a smile.

Terry nodded sympathetically, although she wasn't sure what to make of his last remark. She glanced down at her own chipped nails.

"Yeah, it's the same in my field. The digging class is always getting exploited by the bosses. Even the archaeologists who claim to be radical are really part of the system. Marxism is just another theoretical model to them. Another way of interpreting their sites. It's not real politics."

Manuel looked up from his own excavation and gave an inquiring grunt.

"What do you mean, sister? You saying archaeologists don't believe their own theories? And what does Marxism have to do with archaeology? Or real life, for that matter?" he added.

"Well, that's not quite what I meant." Terry screwed up her face to show she was serious. "Are you interested?" Receiving a noncommittal shrug, she went on.

"I learned early on that archaeologists are like the Viking raiders. Only instead of hitting villagers for their cattle and treasure, we go raiding other disciplines for theories about how society works and the forces that hold it together."

Manuel grinned, the first hint of animation his companion had noticed in him.

"That'd be a wild scene: A bunch of old anthro profs sneaking over to the sociology department, grabbing what they can, and hightailing it back down to the second floor."

"Weeell, it's not exactly like that. But a bunch of the theoretical models we use, like Marxism, didn't come from within anthropology, and most of the influential thinkers aren't anthropologists, let alone archaeologists."

"You mean the French guys. Foucault, Bourdieu, and the rest. I never could keep them straight."

"You're not alone there. But don't worry about them. The most important thing to remember is that Karl Marx was first and foremost a *revolutionary*."

An intensity passed over Terry's face as she spoke the word, and her voice became gruff.

"He saw that something was wrong with nineteenth-century Western

THE CONTENTS OF KARL MARX'S BRAIN
(abridged version)

UNCLE KARL'S first idea:

MATERIALISM is the notion that the physical necessities of life are far more important than what we think. STUFF is more important than IDEAS, and the desire to accumulate stuff leads to CONFLICT.

UNCLE KARL'S second idea:

CONFLICT is the usual state of affairs in non-egalitarian societies as those in power try to keep it. They do this by BRUTE FORCE and by creating a supportive IDEOLOGY.

UNCLE KARL'S 3rd idea:

IDEOLOGY—the set of BELIEFS people have about the world—is determined by the ECONOMIC SYSTEM people live under, not the other way around. So, there's no such thing as "objective" HISTORY.

UNCLE KARL'S 4th idea:

HISTORY (and archaeology, too) is political because it involves interpreting the past from some perspective. You just can't write history— or interpret an archaeological site—without taking a POLITICAL stance, whether you want to or not.

Marx had lots of interesting ideas about the way the world works... but plenty of people don't believe him.

Do you take revolution with your archaeology, sir?

Do you mean that some old prof who doesn't know if it's Monday or Thursday is engaging in political action whenever he interprets his site?

Yes -- according to Uncle Karl, anyway.
He would say that the old geezer either **recognizes** the class conflicts that created "his" data or he **ignores** them. Either way, he is taking a position.

The idea that archaeologists should think about all of the **political** implications of their work got a lot of people thinking that the field should have **social goals**, rather than being just a pastime for intellectuals.

And that led to some of the approaches we call **post-processual**.

118

society. That there were incredible inequities in wealth and power. And he wanted to fix it. But to fix it, he had to understand it. And that meant developing a model of the conditions that created the social structure of the time. I'm saying that he was only interested in history and sociology as the means to an end: revolution!

"Uncle Karl's basic idea, his greatest insight, was this: The owners of the means of production have different and irreconcilable interests from the proletariat, the ordinary folks who work for them. Basically, he said the owners want to get everything they can out of their workers to create wealth. Meanwhile, the workers want to maximize their own power to take back some of the wealth they've created. And, what's more, he thought this relationship was so clear that unless the owners could confuse it in the minds of the proletariat, revolution was inevitable. According to Uncle Karl, this is the source of institutions like religion that create what he called a *false consciousness* in the mind of the non-property-owning classes."

"Sure, I can see that," said Manuel, getting into the swing of things. "If you think you'll get your reward when you're dead, you won't pay much attention to how badly you're being treated here on earth. I guess the trick is to convince the herd that it's really true and that the way society is organized—with me on the top and the rest on the bottom—is just the way it should be. But I don't see what it has to do with archaeology or interning."

"Then I'll give you an example. There's a guy called Sean who works here. He's a **shovelbum**—an archaeologist who makes his living by moving around from site to site. The other day I was trying to raise his political consciousness. I asked him why he thought he gets paid about ten dollars an hour while professors and company owners and the people he works for make a hell of a lot more and get vacation pay and sick days off. And Sean said that he supposed it's because they are better at the job than he is. They know more about archeology than he does. He doesn't want to be a shovelbum forever, so he says he's going to grad school so he can get to be a higher-up himself. His bosses keep telling him that being a field technician isn't a long-term occupation. If you want to get anywhere you have to get some degrees after your name, they say.

"Now, Uncle Karl would say that the idea that being a shovelbum is only a temporary stopping-off point on the road to becoming a professor or a company owner is a myth that's perpetuated to . . ."

". . . to create a false consciousness and justify paying someone with a BA and experience ten dollars an hour. Yeah, I get it."

"How many jobs for professors of archaeology do you think there are in this country? A handful, compared with the number of frikkin' PhDs running around. And the same goes for real, permanent jobs with contract archaeology companies. Twenty-five years ago there may have been no place for a permanent class of low-level field archaeologists, but it's certainly not the case today. Since CRM came along, archaeology isn't just done in the summer vacations, so students aren't a reliable source of labor. The archaeological consultants couldn't survive without experienced, full-time field-workers like Sean and all the others. I've run into quite a few diggers who've been going from job to job for years. Which is all right until your back goes out or you get arthritis in the knees or carpal tunnel syndrome from typing site record forms on a laptop computer for weeks on end."

"And the same goes for a guy like me," said Manuel with enthusiasm. "Being an intern is like slave labor."

There was a roll of forced laughter from behind the truck.

"Are you going to lead us in a chorus of "The Red Flag" now, Theresa?" came Ian Tuliver's unmistakable drawl as he sauntered into view from behind the truck. "Surely you don't really believe academe is merely a pawn in some kind of Kafkaesque plot. Do we promise our students a life on easy street as a reward for their attempts at scholarship? I think not," he concluded in the tone used by physicians of the old school for their patients and others of limited mental capacity.

"I was just making the point," said Terry through her teeth, "that from a Marxist perspective, knowledge is just another commodity that's bought and sold like automobiles, oil futures, or . . ." She scouted around for another example as Tuliver ambled past.

"Or ladies' hair products?" he suggested carelessly over his shoulder.

The skin at the roots of Terry's own dye job turned crimson, her work-hardened fists clenched, and, if profanity could kill, it would have been all over for Ian Tuliver. Instead, he strolled off down the trail with a wave. Evidently, an important fax was waiting for him back at the dig's office. Tuliver doubted he'd bother to return. The Germanic manners of that photographer were too much to bear; and besides, the cameo shot with his Washington Venus had already been taken.

Terry's heart rate was still as rapid as a sprinter's, and it seemed like only a few seconds had gone by since Tuliver disappeared into the woods, when the photographer himself ran up to the truck, his loaded vest thumping against his hips. Ignoring the archaeologist, he grabbed Manuel by the shoulders and dragged him to his feet.

"Now. Quickly, Manoo-al," he declared. "Herr Tulifer is left. Unload the boxes. Lay out the costumes. Quick, I say. We get the shoot done before . . . we get it done right quick and have beers, huh?" He gave Manuel an exaggerated wink, slapped him on the back, and dashed off into the gloom.

Terry slipped down from the truck's tailgate.

"You know, Manuel," said she, "your boss has such a strong accent, it almost sounded like he said *lay out the costumes.*"

After a few moments of silence, she stepped a little closer.

"Manuel? I said it sounded like *costumes.*"

A grin slowly appeared on the young man's face.

"It's like I said, sister. You gotta have a sense of humor when you ride with Hans Wurst."

Hannah worked solidly all afternoon and into the evening and now had "G Is for Gender" virtually in the bag. The dungeonlike atmosphere of her room was claustrophobic, to be sure, but its lack of charm had compensations in the lack of distractions.

It had been a joyously productive day. Hannah was completely focused on her work, entirely unaware that in the world outside, the sun was sinking below the hills and shadows were growing long. And that a form crept furtively out of the woods and was at that very moment making its way along the building to the very window of her bathroom, its glass pane still broken.

As Hannah struggled to think of a synonym for *profligate*, a hand reached inside and unlatched the window, pushing it ajar and slicing some skin on a jagged shard of glass.

A droplet of crimson slid down the pane.

While Hannah mused on **epistemology**, someone hauled his body headfirst through the window and dropped to the floor with hardly a sound. The room was almost completely dark, lit only by a band of light that glowed pale under the door. The blood-streaked hand gingerly pulled the door open a crack. Instantly it flew into his face, throwing him backward. Hannah burst through the door in a flash, pinning the intruder facedown on the floor. His left arm drawn up behind his back almost to the point of dislocation, the beleaguered interloper shrieked in agony.

At the sound of the invader's voice, Hannah released her grip.

"Sean. You idiot," she snapped angrily, helping her poor nephew upright. "In another moment I would have broken your arm."

"No kidding." Sean stretched his poor limb, massaging the wrist that had been so cruelly wrenched into such an unnatural angle.

"What the hell do you expect?" she demanded a little more gently. "Climbing through people's windows after dark. What are you up to?"

"Tuliver and that guy Bott were talking out on the porch, and I didn't want to run into them, so I thought . . ." His voice trailed off pathetically and he looked up at her, puppy like, nursing his injured paw.

"Do stop looking at me like that!" said Hannah briskly, but not unkindly. She took his uninjured wrist, hoisted Sean onto his feet, and led him out of the bathroom. He had never imagined that his aunt was so strong. But of course that isn't the kind of speculation in which a man of twenty-three usually engages in relation to middle-aged female relatives.

She sat in the only chair and threw Sean a pillow, motioning him to take a place on the floor at her feet.

"I think I may board up that bathroom," said Hannah. "Seems to be a portal to the twilight zone. Well, boychik?"

Hannah folded her arms on her chest and fixed Sean with the stern look of the wronged party.

At this point your author draws a veil of discretion over the proceedings. For he is unwilling to pander to the voyeuristic inclinations of the depraved or to offend the delicate sensibilities of the impressionable. There shall be no description of Sean's pitiful appearance, his forlorn and heartbroken sobs, and his dramatic howls against the mindless cruelty of fate.

Freya and he had had a spat.

"And it's your fault, too," sniffled Sean. "Well, sort of."

"My fault?" Hannah shot back more in surprise than anger. "I've never even met the girl."

"Well, it's not *exactly* your fault. She, Magnus, and me'd been talking about how the bones were stolen, and he was saying how terrible it was."

"So the Children of Zeus didn't do it?" asked Hannah.

"Odin. Children of Odin. And, no, they didn't. At least, that's what Magnus said. Anyway, somehow we got around to talking about who might have taken them, and we were listing all the people on the island. Including you."

"Thanks for the confidence."

"We were just making a list. So anyway, Freya started calling you 'Nana.' And I said that your name was Hannah with an *H*, but that you said it with that throaty '*ch*' sound. And Magnus asked what kind of a name that was. And I said Israeli. And that's when things started getting weird."

Hannah leaned toward her nephew and began to turn her bracelets as she did when thinking hard. "Weird? How do you mean, weird?"

"Well, he kinda started cross-questioning me."

"About?"

"About our family and granddad and stuff. And Magnus asked if he was Jewish, and I said that was pretty much required for a cantor. And then he started going on about how the Jews are not really descended from Abraham. And how the northern Europeans are really the chosen people, and it just got real strange. It was almost, like, anti-Semitic. And the worst part was that Freya didn't say a word. She just stood there. Oh, Hannah, what's it about?" he implored.

"I'm so sorry that you've had your eyes opened like this, Sean." She reached down and squeezed the shoulder of her sister's sentimental offspring.

"I know you think history is pretty much just an interesting pastime, and that what people think about the past doesn't really matter too much. Just a bunch of professors playing intellectual games for their own amusement. And maybe some of it is. But not all. You've just found out that how we interpret the past and the stories we tell about past realities have real effects on what we think about ourselves and other people.

"When most white people in South Africa believed that their ancestors settled an unpopulated wilderness instead of a land inhabited by the Xhosas and the Bantus, don't you think that supported the policy of apartheid? It's the same with the Children of Odin. They've used some kind of twisted scholarship to convince themselves that white people are God's chosen. And, of course, that makes some other groups slightly less than human. In a much less extreme way, there's a parallel with archaeologists who interpret sites using models that emphasize the natural environment, or class and gender struggles, or whatever and really *believe* they are seeing the total reality—that one force is behind everything they see in the **archaeological record**."

"You can bring archaeology into just about any situation, can't you?"

"Yes," she grinned. "I'm hopelessly twisted that way. Just can't help trying to see pattern in human behavior. And if you had an intellectual problem, boychik, we could work through it rationally. But intellectualizing doesn't always help. You need someone who can come up with a plan. Someone who can play Friar Laurence to your Romeo."

"Didn't Romeo and Juliet end up dead? Thanks, Hannah, but I'm not that far gone!"

"Well, in my humble opinion Dr. Tuliver should never have approved this . . . this charade," said Alasdair peevishly.

His sackcloth jerkin and leggings itched, and the strip of leather he had been given for a belt kept getting loose, threatening to send his pants to the ground. It was incredible that Tuliver would have agreed to them dressing up like Neolithic peasants for that photographer. And it was shocking that a magazine like the *International Geographic* would go in for this sort of playacting.

"Well at least you don't have to wear a sheet and bow to the frikkin' goddess," replied Terry. "I feel like I'm at First Communion. And the thing's coming apart at the seams."

The four pseudo-Neolithic villagers huddled inside the finds tent in various stages of embarrassment, outrage, and amusement as Hans Wurst's crew gathered up the equipment in preparation for the second shoot of the evening, this one down at the tower.

Facing away from the group, Sandra was reengineering her bodice to get the best out of her less-than-extravagant chest.

"You two are taking it all too seriously," said she. "Really. I think it's fun dressing up like . . . whatever it is we're supposed to be. Like Hans said, photographs are more interesting with people in them. I wonder if we'll get royalties. Did everyone sign a release?"

At sixteen, Sandra had done a screen test for a horror-on-the-beach movie. Although she had not been called back, she thought of herself as a Hollywood initiate. Attractive and photogenic, she wasn't ashamed to admit that she enjoyed it.

Terry grunted. "You're wasting your time with that bodice, Sandra. They're not interested in your cleavage."

"Even if they could find it."

Terry gave a catlike hiss. "Ouch. That was mean, Alasdair. But I thought you liked them skinny. Seem to remember that Miss Ten O'Clock News was built like a poster girl for frikkin' anorexia."

A caustic reply began to form in Alasdair's mind, but he thought better of it as the silent, hulking figure of Big Dave began to stir in his seat.

Of the four, Dave looked most authentic and seemed at ease in his rustic costume, although this may have had something to do with the nips he frequently took from a leather-covered flask. It didn't take much imagination to see him in the role of a sturdy Neolithic farmer enlisted by his chieftain to haul stones for some ancient megalithic monument, which was how he was cast in the photo session earlier that evening.

Alasdair stood up, hiked up his loose trousers, and tightened his belt.

"We'd better be heading down to the tower for the next performance. Where did you put the lanterns, Dave?"

"Perhaps we'll run into the old guy with the mysterious rocks," suggested Sandra. "Sean said he has, like, a camp down there somewhere."

"No, no. He's left," said Alasdair a little too rapidly. "At least, that's what I heard."

With kerosene lanterns in front and rear, the group set out in single file along the woodland path whose right-hand fork would lead them to the tower. To their only observer, an elderly woman in a broad-brimmed hat, the costumed figures brought back memories of this place long ago. She shed a tear of remembrance and followed at a distance, needing no light to guide her feet.

"Wait up a bit, Dave," said Terry after ten minutes. "This goddamned sheet is coming apart again." For the fourth time, she turned away and adjusted the safety pins at her shoulder.

"I suppose," said Alasdair from his position in the rear, "to *some* people here, all this crap is an acceptable research strategy. Just another way to interpret the archaeological data, huh, Dave?"

"Postmodern bullshit," snapped Terry. She had no respect for her large colleague's theoretical orientation. And the way he hung around her got on her nerves—mostly—although she didn't like to see him picked on by Alasdair, who was always ready with a mean comment.

"For once I agree with you, Terry."

"Don't break out the frikkin' champagne," said Terry over her shoulder. "Just because I don't go along with that fuzzy postmodern crud doesn't mean your brand of environmental determinism makes any sense."

From the back of the line, Alasdair let out what he hoped was an amused laugh.

"For your information, Sandra, that was a typical Marxist response to the clear logic of the ecological approach. For some reason they just refuse to give hunter-foragers and simple agriculturists credit for being rational human beings."

"Oh yeah?" said Sandra, feeling that the remark needed some reply.

"I was referring to optimal foraging theory. Perhaps you've heard of it? It's simply a way of understanding how hunter-foragers go about deciding what kinds of foods they'll use most. And of course that'll influence their settlement pattern and their social structure. To be brief . . ."

"Another unlikely concept," rumbled Dave. He took another hit from the flask.

". . . people will maximize the quantity of resources they accumulate by working out which type of food—salmon, for example—they can get with the smallest amount of effort. Think of it this way: in the summer, it makes more sense to spend two days fishing and getting enough salmon to feed me for a week than it would to spend a week trying to collect seeds that might only last a couple of days. Optimal foraging theory predicts that people make the judgment whether or not the food value of a particular resource is worth the effort it takes to find it and get it ready to eat."

Sandra shrugged, not caring much either way. "What-ever."

"Yeah, yeah, yeah," said Terry, stopping the line again to take out a safety pin that was poking her in the shoulder.

"No one's saying that prehistoric people didn't have to eat. But it's a hell of a jump from there to speculating about their motivations. Rationally optimizing resources, were they? Huh! All you're doing, Alasdair, is projecting the values of your own modern, capitalist society back into the past. According to you, everyone in prehistory was always ruled by the desire to accumulate things. Resources, commodities, wealth, profit. You've just created a past in the image of the present. A typical strategy to naturalize the status quo. To 'prove' that capitalist attitudes are just a natural part of the human being and human history and our place in the natural environment. That's just frikkin' bull!"

Terry looked up and raised her hands to the sky, as if asking for divine help in the extremity of her frustration. How could Alasdair be so dense?

"Everything's political with you people, isn't it?" he retorted. "Can't you conceive of any *other* influences on society and culture? Doesn't the natural environment have any role? In my humble opinion, the trouble with you neo-Marxists and critical theorists is that you only have one idea. And that one explanation fits every situation. Whatever happened in the past, it *must* be due to power struggles between interest groups."

As they squared off, the little group had come to a complete standstill among the high bushes that lined the coastal path. Alasdair was standing calmly holding his lantern, while Terry gestured with a passion that frequently caused the left shoulder strap on her costume to slide over her brown shoulder and Big Dave to look on appreciatively.

"Of course people have to eat," she declared. "But social change happens for *social* reasons! As soon as people organize themselves to survive in their environment—adapt, if you prefer that word—they create social structure. And where you have social structure, there's hierarchy. With some groups taking more of the resources because they have the power. Politics wasn't invented by lefty academics. Its been a part of human life since there was society."

Alasdair shook his head. How frustrating this was. Terry had completely missed the point.

"Fine," he said. "I'm not denying that. But it doesn't help us to understand social change as well as environmental models do. In the Neolithic, for example." He poked his thumb over his shoulder back toward the site.

"What? Are you frikkin' nuts?" Terry hit her forehead with the palm of her hand, causing the loose strap to dive south once again. "There's a million articles on the Neolithic. What about Tilley's work in Sweden that we read last term? What's your humble opinion about that?"

Alasdair kept quiet and put on a superior expression. The truth was he'd skimmed the article and remembered next to nothing.

"As you *may* remember, Tilley was trying to explain changes in burial rituals that happened during the middle Neolithic, about 4,000 to 4,500 years ago, in southern Sweden. In the earlier period, what he called the *Funnel Neck Beaker Tradition* or TRB, burial rituals were very complex. The people would use the tombs over and over again. They'd crush lots of pottery vessels at the entrance to the tomb and mix up the bones of the people who were already buried there into piles. Burial rituals got even more complex as time went on, when suddenly everything changed: In the period Tilley called *BAC*—short for "Battle-Axe / Corded Ware Tradition"—the people stopped making the great offerings of pottery, and started to bury just one person in each burial barrow. Basically, there was a whole lot less emphasis on ritual and the conspicuous destruction of wealth objects. Is any of this familiar?"

Alasdair ignored Terry's taunt. He'd never been able to remember the stupid acronyms.

"Tilley thought this reflected a change in power relations within these groups. He started out with the premise that social inequalities are very clear to people who live in small, lineage-based societies like the folk of the Swedish Neolithic. To keep everyone toeing the line, the group in charge has to legitimize its position by convincing the rest that their social structure is a part of the natural order. That it can't or shouldn't change. Tilley said the group in power used rituals associated with death and burial to support this ideology. The chambered tombs are massively impressive and scary. And they are links to both the group's past and the spirit world. So the powerful group keeps the secret ritual knowledge to itself. During a burial, they destroy wealth objects to make the event more memorable to the people who are watching. Then they mix up the bones to show that there's no lasting difference in social status between members of the community—even though there obviously is!

"According to Tilley, the differences in wealth and power within the communities became so extreme that this kind of legitimization wasn't enough. The power of the lineages declined, and the communities became more egalitarian, as shown by the simpler burial practices of the BAC period."

"Fine. So what's your point?"

"The point is that exploitative social structures don't just keep going by momentum. They have to be maintained by ideologies that support the powerful. So when I look at a chambered tomb, I see ideology and the process of social reproduction—the way the powerful actively use artifacts and ritual to keep people thinking their power is natural and right."

"Hmm. No truck," observed Alasdair as the tower came into view. "I bet those photographers and their idiot driver got lost."

Terry chewed on her lip and pulled the robe more tightly around her against the chill. She had told Manuel not to take the supposed shortcut across the meadow below the site, but he had laughed her off. What could a girl know about driving trucks?

Although Terry didn't know it, her prediction had been right. Only half an hour earlier, Manuel had bounced the heavy rig down onto the meadow and straight into a patch of marshy ground. Soon it was hopelessly stuck, wheels slinging mud into the air with wild impotence and digging in deeper with every rotation.

"Ach! Screw it," Hans had bellowed. "We leave the thing here and come back tomorrow."

He slammed his fist on the dashboard and instantly forgot all about the costumed archaeologists who were awaiting him a little farther down the road.

The tower was impressive in the failing light. Solidly built of local stone, it rose squarely above the surrounding brush. The stonework was cunningly laid to resemble the masonry of a medieval church or castle, with an arch above each narrow window and a crenellated parapet. Alasdair lifted the heavy, old-fashioned latch, and the door swung noiselessly open. The smell of sulfur emanated from white plastic bags of fertilizer that were stacked in a corner and under the open staircase.

And something else. A sweet, sickening odor of decay.

While Alasdair remained outside, cautiously holding the door open, Terry and Dave with his lantern stepped inside.

"Phew! Smells like something came in here to die," said Terry, holding her nose. "Looks like this was a kitchen and . . ."

She stopped in midstream, and Big Dave felt a hand grab his sleeve. With a quick reaction he was able to stop her from falling hard.

"Whoa! That was like tripping on a banana skin."

Setting Terry back on her feet, Dave scouted around for the offending object that she had kicked back toward the door. He crouched and poked at it with a stick, and swallowed hard. The slimy object was covered with globs of blood and yellow masses that he recognized as fat. The floor was streaked with dried blood and pieces of animal tissue. Now the source of the putrid smell was clear. He stood up, unsure whether to explain the discovery to Terry.

But she had not moved—she was frozen, staring ahead at a rough table that stood across from the doorway. As Dave turned his lantern to the rear wall, he could see the reason for her horror. Cascading over the table's edge hung several feet of bloody entrails. The stink hit her nostrils, and Terry let out a shriek. Alasdair and Sandra rushed inside to help, and the great door swung closed behind them with a thump.

Terry stepped gingerly toward the scene of carnage. Several small, disembodied heads lay upon the table, their fur and long ears matted into bloody clumps.

"It's OK," cried Terry in relief. "It's only that frikkin' Rock Man. He's been butchering rabbits. Phew, what a stink. Let's get the hell outta here."

"Hate to tell you guys," said Big Dave, pushing at the door with enough force to move a small rhinoceros, "but there's a minor impediment to that plan. Because unless I'm wrong, Alasdair the Boy Wonder has just locked us in!"

The shock was palpable.

No one had ever heard Dave utter a sentence that long before.

"N" IS FOR NEOEVOLUTIONISM, AND "A" IS FOR AGENCY

In Which the Crew Adapt to Their Environment

S tinky water had seeped into her boots and made her socks squeak and slosh with every step, but Freya couldn't care less. She had wandered around in a daze for hours after the awful scene at the last ritual, and had ended up back at camp near the old Skunk Point lighthouse.

Had someone followed her some of the way through the woods? Probably just dumb paranoia. Whatever. At this point she didn't really care.

Feeling abandoned and stupid, she plopped down on a rock, her chin in her hands. The camp was deserted except for her own tent. Some rectangles of flattened grass showed where the others had stood. The ring of stones they used for the campfire had the same half-burned logs that the group had been trying to ignite for days now. Too big and too green, of course, but the smell of damp, burned wood lingered. All in all, it was a pretty dismal scene.

Freya gave a deep sigh and shifted her seat. The damp was coming through her jeans, and she was starting to feel her poor feet.

This whole Norse thing had been a mistake. The Children of Odin had plenty of ideas, but after her talk with Sean their dogma seemed, well, a bit racist, what with their obsession with purity and talk of the coming race war. All this stuff was a million miles from the Wiccan principle of "an it harm none, do what ye will," and Freya had decided that this was definitely not the group for her. The only thing that kept her on the island, her only commitment, was the carving of the goddess. That was something real. A connection to ancient times. She felt that something good was bound to happen if she just kept faith with the ancient Law of Three: the energy you put into the world comes back threefold—for good or for bad.

The carving was one good thing, of course. And then meeting Sean just as she was meditating on the goddess. Was that just luck? No way. Then there was that unforgettable night at the archaeological site . . .

But then it had all started to go wrong. Who'd stolen the bones? Not the Children of Odin, she knew that. Magnus had been so angry when he had heard about it. He thought the archaeologists had done it just to keep the bones for themselves. But that wasn't true either.

Just look at how they had treated Sean, she'd said.

No, insisted Magnus. They were just trying to trick her. And then he had come up with all that creepy stuff about Sean's family. Man, it had been a real mistake to tell Magnus her boyfriend's story. It had just opened the gates of high weirdness.

Boyfriend. Was that what he was? Definitely not. When two people do it under the eye of the goddess, they make something real between them. They make a bond. They make . . .

Oh, oh . . .

Freya swallowed hard, thinking of something else they might have made.

Up she jumped, and, brushing off the seat of her pants, she started sprinting west along the coast path. Sean was probably at the old school. She'd see him. She'd find out what was going on between them.

Terry held her nose. "Phew, that stinks, man!"

"Now tell us something we don't know."

"Up yours, Alasdair. You're the one who locked us in here." They glared at each other for a few seconds before Terry turned away with a sniff.

"Well, I'm going to do something useful. Like try to find a way out of here," she said.

The tower room was about twenty feet square, with a massive stone fireplace set into the wall opposite the door. On Terry's right, wooden stairs led up, and there were window slits wide enough to let in some light—but high up, and too narrow for an eight year old. No chance of getting through there.

She started cautiously up the stairs. Staying close to the wall, she made her way up until an ominous creak showed that things were not as sturdy as they looked. She backed down carefully. There was a ripping sound as her robe caught on a nail.

"Goddammit! This frikkin' robe thing is hooked. There, it's free again. I'm coming down. These stairs aren't safe."

"What now, then?" she asked. "We can't go up, and we can't get out of the window, and *someone* closed the frikkin' door, so that's no good."

"Ah, could we, like, light a fire or something?" asked Sandra. She nodded toward the fireplace. "Someone might see the smoke and . . . something," she trailed off.

"Kill ourselves with the fumes, more likely," sniffed Alasdair. "Can't you see that the hearth's just for show? There's no chimney—you know, the thing that takes away the smoke? Or don't they have chimneys in SoCal?"

"Did anyone check to see if there's cell phone service?"

They groped in bags and pockets.

"Nope."

"Nada."

"No service."

"No phone," said Dave.

"Wait a minute," said Sandra. "Check this out. I've got an alarm app on my iPhone." She poked a button and held the gadget up to the window. There were the opening electric cords of a popular song.

"Whoops, sorry. Wrong app. Here. This is the one."

It began with the wail of a siren, changed to a series of short discords, and then went back to the wail. And it was loud.

"Sounds like a car alarm," shouted Terry over the row.

"Very useful," said Alasdair. "When was the last time anyone took notice of a car alarm?" After a minute, he said, "Turn the stupid thing off. No one's coming, and it's giving me a headache."

But just as Sandra was going to protest, there came the sound of someone rattling the great wooden door and a shout.

"Anyone in there?"

All the prisoners yelled at once, and after some pushing and pulling the door swung open. A waft of fresh air blew in, and the team blinked in the light.

"Heard your noise. What are you-all doin'?" said Freya. Seeing Sandra, she didn't wait for a reply. "Sean here?" she demanded, eyeing the other as if she were going to throw something.

"Ah, no," said Sandra. "I've no idea where he is. We've been . . ."

The door slammed shut, and they heard the latch click.

"Goddammit! We're locked in again," spat Terry, and she slapped the wall in frustration. "What the hell do we do now?"

Silence.

"That was your fault," said Alasdair, stabbing a finger in Sandra's direction. "You made her angry."

"Not fair," whimpered the girl. She hugged the robe around her and sniffed. "That's how she's been every time I've seen her. Don't know why she thinks I'm, like, interested in Sean."

Alasdair gave a snort.

"Competition for scarce resources is at the root of most human behavior."

"But I'm not in competition for him."

"She still slammed the door 'cause you pissed her off," said Terry.

"But I'm not responsible for that. I didn't do anything."

"Course not! Haven't you learned anything in your theory classes? Individuals just get caught up in these big historical processes. It's like Marx said . . ."

Alasdair groaned. "I thought we'd done with him in back in chapter 8."

"He said that people make history, but they don't control it as individuals."

"Didn't he say that 'men' make history?"

"Shut up, Alasdair. All *you* can make is that squeaky noise with your mouth."

"But," said Sandra quietly, "aren't you're both, like, talking about the same thing, really?

"How's that?" said Dave, who had been sipping at a flask and was feeling quite warm and talkative.

"About how individuals make long-term changes. In culture and history, I mean. That's what the neoevolutionists are trying to work out."

Since her conversation with Hannah back at the old school—it seemed like a decade ago—Sandra had been doing some reading. She quickly discovered that anthropologists hadn't just given up on the relationship between humans and their environment. It turned out that neoevolutionary anthropology was a long way from Alasdair's environmental determinism, in which nature pulls the string and humankind jumps.

"Er, yes," responded the Boy Wonder. "That's right. What you said. Spencer and Darwin."

He was snatching at names only dimly remembered. Alasdair was outside his comfort zone but wasn't going to let those other bozos know it. He was still Dr. Tuliver's right-hand man, and that gave him a certain status. Or so he thought.

"Well, from what I read it's more like Spencer *or* Darwin," said Sandra. "**Herbert Spencer** . . ."

"What kinda name's Herbert?" snorted Terry.

"I guess nineteenth-century English people thought it was, like, OK. He was one of the people who applied Charles Darwin's idea of biological adaptation to human society. Only he saw it as **progress** from lower forms of society to higher forms. The lower ones were simple, and the higher ones were more complex. He came up with the idea of the "survival of the fittest," not Darwin. And he thought that natural selection would just naturally lead, in a kind of step-by-step way, to societies that were more advanced than the ones that came before."

"Like the old Three Ages idea," said Terry. "That people went from stone to bronze to iron. And each one was better than the one before. And of course the prize at the end of the day was that they'd become like civilized Europeans. The very pinnacle of an advanced society. But of course, that's all crud."

"Yeah," went on Sandra. "But the idea was very big in the nineteenth century."

"Sure. It justified all sorts of invasions and national takeovers. If you believe that in dominating some African country you are actually doing them a favor by helping them reach the next step on the ladder of progress, well then, you can rationalize any kind of imperialism."

"More Marxist bunk," said Alasdair.

"And Spencer thought that complexity was the key to progress," went on Sandra. "That as time goes by, organisms and societies both get more complex. A few billion years ago there were, like, only like these simple, squiggly bug things. But now there are elephants and people and stuff. In the past, there were simple societies, but now there are state societies. It's like the more complex something is, the more 'fit' it is."

"More bunk" said Terry.

"That's what the biologists say, too. Spencer got that piece wrong, but a lot of people in England and the U.S.A. still liked what he had to say. It made them feel good about their own culture. But Darwin didn't say anything about complexity being inevitable. That's what Dr. Green said, anyway."

"But surely," whined Alasdair, "you can see there is a natural progression—I won't call it progress—toward more complex societies? The Maya didn't start out building pyramids and all that. If you'd done research, you'd know."

"**Wikipedia** don't count as research, Al," said Big Dave.

"The Maya?" questioned Sandra. "Didn't Colin Renfrew write about them?"

"Of course he did," sniffed Alasdair. "The Maya were a very technologically advanced and socially complex culture. They worked out a stable relationship between their population and the natural resources. An equilibrium that lasted for maybe two thousand years. They had complex buildings, a written language, mathematics, and so on."

"But didn't that all collapse?" put in Sandra. "That's what Renfrew said, anyway. The Maya civilization sort of plodded along until their agricultural system degraded the natural environment. They couldn't grow enough food to support themselves. So their big complex civilization, like, collapsed. Right? That's what Dr. Green said."

"Er, yes." Alasdair didn't like the direction this was going.

"And there are still plenty of Maya people around, right?"

Alasdair stood up and stretched, instead of answering.

"So Maya society sort of adapted to the changing environment by getting simpler. Isn't that right?"

"I suppose so," he grunted.

"Well, that's how the neoevolutionists see it, anyway," said Sandra. "Dr. Green said that . . ."

"I'm getting a bit tired of hearing what she has to say."

". . . they get around what she called *determinism* by looking at how complex the relationship is between culture, environment, and a group's history. The neo-evos start with the assumption that societies adapt—that they have to, or they'd die out. And they think adaptation accounts for a lot of the big changes in societies."

"Big as in . . . ?" asked Dave.

"Well, like when chiefdoms change to states. Power in chiefdoms is based on kinship relations—how I'm related to you and the people we know. But in state societies, your relatives are only one factor. Why did some chiefdoms become kingdoms? The neo-evos think they can understand these big important questions. And work out why modern society's structured the way it is. That's pretty important, huh?"

"Of course," said Alasdair, sounding bored. "And nobody would argue with that. But how are these neoevolutionary types any different from the theorists who came before 'em? I mean, from what you say it's all a matter of adaptation."

"Well, like, Dr. Green says . . ."

"Pleeeze!"

". . . it's because they bring in historical factors. They look at how groups influence their own history. They have like, **agency**."

Terry got up from the floor and fanned her face with her hands.

"Phew. It's getting really stinky in here."

"Yeah, you've said that before."

"I'm trying the stairs again," she said.

Staying close to the side of the staircase and gripping the robe tight around her, Terry crept up to the next level. The air was fresher here. She found a window cut into the stone wall and breathed deeply. And opposite the window, a door. She gave it a push. Locked or jammed. Damn. Up and up she went. The stairs seemed quite sturdy now, and the windows let in plenty of light, although the sun was well on its downward journey. Another window and door, shut like the other. Now she was at the top, and it looked like a dead end. But wait . . .

"Get up here, you guys!" she yelled.

Driven upward to escape the stench of decaying rabbit, and with Big Dave in the lead, the archaeologists climbed the staircase. Soon his lantern illuminated a trapdoor leading out to the roof. They clambered out, and Alasdair placed the lantern carefully on the top of the parapet as a beacon. The entire island stretched out below them, and over to the west the top of the old school building peeped up from the trees. Under different circumstances, it would have been quite picturesque. But with the sun going down, the group huddled below the wall, their only protection from the breeze blowing the first wisps of fog inland.

"Well, so much for that idea," complained Alasdair. "We were better off down with the smell."

"At least Terry showed some agency," said Big Dave. "Like Sandra was saying."

"Huh?"

"Agency theory, dumb-ass," said Terry.

Alasdair waved his hand vaguely, as if to say, "Well of course, *I* know that."

"All that agency stuff is pretty self-evident, in my humble opinion," he went on. "It's nothing but recognizing that people make decisions that affect larger events. Nothing hard about that."

AGENCY AND CHANGE

Why do cultures change?
There's no easy answer to that one, of course. But one of the BIG theoretical discussions is about the role of **human agency** in change.

Are people entirely in charge of their history?
➤ *The Great Man idea*

Are we so hemmed in by human institutions and our environment that we are basically helpless?
➤ *The Process & Structure idea*

Can people change the future by conscious action?
➤ *The Agency in context idea*

THE GREAT MAN?

THE MAN

Extreme belief in human **agency** led to the idea (thankfully a bit out of fashion) that "history is the biography of Great Men". Thomas Carlyle wrote that in 1841.

He meant that the trajectory of history is decided by the people (OK, the Men) who are in **power**. They sit around and make **decisions** that others have to carry out. Build this, invade that, worship the other. They say it and it gets done.

➤ They're Great because they are influential.

AGENCY

THISAWAY THATAWAY
MY WAY WHATEVER

Neoevolutionists picked up on on the idea of agency. And they liked the **Darwinian** model because it explains the general trends of human prehistory. But if you expect that cultures will *always* make the evolutionarily adaptive decision you'll be disappointed.

And this is where they part from the law-and-order **structuralists**: they recognize that human beings are, well, human. History is full of incomprehensible decisions made by the Great and the the not so great.

PROCESS AND STRUCTURE

Under this idea human **agency** gets little or no credit for anything much. Between social structure, ideology, biology, and the natural environment, some theorists don't see how individuals can possibly break through to make more than small scale temporary influences.

Between **adaptation** (which goes on regardless of what we want or think we need) and the hardwired structures of the brain that determine how we experience reality, there's no much room for agency, they say.

STRUCTURE
TECHNOLOGY · DEMOGRAPHY · STRUCTURAL HISTORY · POWER · SOCIAL STRUCTURE · RANDOM HEAD-BANGING · 'OTHER STUFF'

"Yes, that's right. The way Dr. Green explained it . . ." Sandra waited for a groan from Alasdair, got it, and went on.

". . . agency means people acting as agents of change in, like, their own lives. They think about what to do next, do it, and affect their own history."

"Well, duh."

"I guess I didn't explain that very well. The idea that individuals can affect history sorta balances the idea that human societies are these, like, big complex machines that are driven by things like environment, economics, and evolutionary pressures. And that people—individual actors—don't have much of role in what direction the society goes. Determinists are OK with all that complexity because all they see are the big patterns in history. They see societies as groups of people who act in culturally predictable ways, determined by the environment or whatever. And that naturally leads to some predictable outcome."

"Naturally," said Alasdair. "Culture is a form of adaptation. So you'd expect a group's decisions to be adaptive in the long run. Cultures develop all manner of institutions like religion, marriage, and social structures to make sure that that happens."

"Right," said Terry. "And the people in power make sure that everyone else keeps the rules. Either by violence or (like Marx said) by convincing everyone that *our* way of doing things is the only sensible way."

"Yeah, and people usually do stick to the rules," went on Sandra. Now that she understood these ideas, it was a lot easier to see where they fit together. "That's why anthropologists can say that cultural behavior is predictable and structured. Societies have, like, norms of behavior, and there's a lot a pressure for individuals to conform. That's a kinda 'law and order' idea of culture, with people living inside a bunch of big, powerful, interconnected structures that make up their society. At least, that's the feeling I got reading the old-time social anthropologists. Then a Brit named Anthony Giddens came up with an idea he called **structuration** . . ."

"Hate those made-up words," said Alasdair.

"He said that we miss a big chunk of reality if we only think about these structures. He said people are pretty much aware that they are cogs in the machine. And they know that to help themselves, they either have to change the rules or get around them. And when they do that, they're using agency. Events have **proximate causes** as well as structural ones. Agency theory helps us remember that things happen by people taking action."

"Hmm. I see what you mean," said Terry. "Change can happen when individuals act in weird, idiosyncratic ways, not just how their culture expects them to. But you can take it too far. Old Thomas Carlyle actually believed that 'history is the story of great men.' Meaning that what we call *history* is just the result of conscious decisions made by a few powerful individuals. Men, of course. What an elitist bozo."

"OK, but on the other extreme are the determinists. To them history is a matter of huge forces working on each other. The way Dr. Green puts it, a theory's useful 'cause it helps us understand why things are the way they are. But some of these models fit one situation better than another. Neoevolutionism is about the adaptive qualities of behavior—but that's only one reason why things happen, and a long-term, large-scale reason, too. It's like trying to explain 'why' my car is running. I could say it's because of the way air and gasoline molecules interact. Or because I turned the key. Or because I want to drive home to feed the cat. They're all right, and none is more right than any of the others.

"In evolutionary terms, religion is just a system that encourages stability and long-term reproductive success for the group. That's true, and it's useful to know. But it doesn't tell you why individual people actually do religion or what it means to them. Theorists come up with generalizations about how societies work. And while they can show us the ultimate outcomes of behavior, they may not be at all useful in understanding life as people live it. Getting at the root cause of something makes any other explanation seem somehow trivial. Like foam on the top of a wave. Until you realize that the foam is everyday life. And that although evolutionary forces are manipulating us at some deep level, people can and do affect the course of their own histories. Without agency, it's all pattern and no people."

"That's a catchy phrase," said Alasdair. "But the whole point of evolution is that the people who have the most efficient adaptation win the prize. That is, they get to replace whatever less efficient group came before them."

"Humph. Al's had a brain freeze. Must be the weather." Dave took another sip from his hip flask.

"Haven't you been listening?" said Terry. "Theory's come a long way since Herbert Spencer, which seems to be where your brain is stuck."

"Yes, yes. Sandra has found her voice. Very good. But what archaeologist has ever actually used these ideas? That's what I want to know."

Alasdair yawned as if to say that he didn't want to know it that much. "And how can you know what people were actually thinking? All are informants are dead, and most didn't write anything down. Brrr. It's hella cold up here."

He snuggled tentatively against Terry.

"I, like, read some articles about Hawai'i that . . ." began Sandra.

"Aww! Don't say it." Alasdair squawked and shuffled back to his place as Terry stuck her elbow in his ribs.

". . . that Dr. Green lent me. Well, maybe I didn't read the whole thing. But I gave it, like, a pretty thorough skim."

"Sounds like science to me," put in Dave.

"Hawai'i is, like, a special case," she went on.

"It's way out there in the middle of the Pacific, and no one lived there until about 1,500 years ago. When Europeans got there in the eighteenth century, Hawaiians had organized themselves into a state. With kings and taxes and monuments and all that. But the cool thing is that they also had oral histories that talked about decisions the kings and chiefs made, and alliances, and all that political stuff you can't get from archaeology. And then there are the accounts of the European explorers. People like Captain Cook, who visited at the end of the eighteenth century. Cook was a good observer and wrote a lot about the people he met, their customs, and their politics."

"Yeah, well," yawned Alasdair, "but how's that so special?"

"Don't you see? It's the only place in the world where there are actual accounts of how a state society came into being. From a series of chiefdoms, I mean. All the famous archaic states that archaeologists like so much—dynastic Egypt and the rest—came and went centuries ago. So there's almost nothing in the way of written records or oral history. Archaeologists had to reconstruct what their societies were like from analogy. But with Hawai'i . . ."

"We have the archaeology *and* the other sources," said Terry. "And here was I thinking that it was just beaches, tall drinks with little umbrellas in them, and tropical sunshine."

143

"Don't say it," moaned Alasdair. "I'll take some of that sunshine right about now. But you seem to have got off track. What has all this to do with agency, neoevolutionism, and all that business?"

"Er, I'm getting there."

Sandra was wishing just about now that she had read Pat Kirch's article a bit more closely. She hadn't been expecting to have to explain his ideas to a bunch of grad students. And certainly not dressed in a sheet on top of a freezing cold tower.

"Well, we have to start with the island biogeography. Part of Hawai'i has wet weather, and part tends to be dry. This meant that they practiced different sorts of agriculture in the different regions. On the wet side they farmed intensively, using all the land as efficiently as they could, and grew a lot of good, storable crops like taro. Soon the wet side had a large population and was pretty prosperous. They built huge temples and public buildings and roads. On the dry side it was all about smaller, weaker crops like sweet potatoes and yams. The people there weren't so well off."

"And they didn't have the taro," put in Terry. "Religious importance, y'know. Their societies had all these religious rules called *tapu* that were enforced by priests. And one had to do with taro. Controlling taro production meant that you controlled part of the relationship between people and the gods. It was part of the way that the kings legitimized themselves as chosen by the gods. So everyone wanted taro."

Sandra went on.

"The islands used to be governed by regional kings. They were kings, remember. Chosen by the gods, like most kings, and supported by a state religion, an army, taxes, and all the rest of that stuff. Each island had several kings, and they were constantly at war with each other. For some reason—I never understood why—the rulers on the dry side were fiercer than the others. Although they didn't have the natural resources, they put their wealth into building stronger armies. They wanted to capture the wetlanders' territory to get more productive land and to take over the taro production. Eventually, the drylanders took control, and by the eighteenth century they had turned the weaker rulers into their vassals. King Kamehameha consolidated all these regional rulers and became, like, the high king."

"But that doesn't make sense," said Alasdair. "The wetland people were more efficient than the others. They used less energy to get more

resources. They should have just out-competed the dryland groups. Just gone up there, killed them, and taken their land. Isn't that what you'd expect, from a Darwinian perspective?"

"Weren't you listening?" broke in Terry. "The historical sources say that isn't what happened. And Sandra's been saying for the last ten minutes that neoevolutionism doesn't suggest that outcomes only happen because of long-term causes. That's why it's so cool that we know all about the local politics and other events that led up to Kamehameha being in power. It means that we can work out both the proximate and the long-term reasons why this kingship developed."

"Such as?"

"Well, none of it would have happened without the cultures that developed under wet and dry agriculture systems. So you could say it came down to biogeography. On the other hand, there were political decisions made by actual people. Captain Cook wrote all about that in his journals. Nothing would have changed without these individuals. They made decisions that affected history, but they did it in this larger context. And there you have agency at work."

Wisps of fog floated by, barely visible in the gloom. Sandra shivered and warmed her hands around the dying lantern. The others seemed to be warming up just by arguing, but as the chill set in she found the discussion less important, considering their predicament. She glanced at her phone. No service, of course.

Damn you, AT&T.

Since Terry had elbowed her way into the discussion and finally stolen her conclusion, Sandra had seriously considered trying to squeeze through one of the window slots or scaling the wall. It was a long way down, but the irregular stones would give her some foothold, she imagined. And she'd rather risk hitting the ground with a splat and getting it over with.

Anything would be better than this never-ending Death by Theory.

Well, perhaps not.

But at least she was going to get off the roof for a while. It was cold, and she needed a bathroom. Perhaps it was behind one of those doors. The others were still talking. At least, Terry was talking. Big Dave just sat grinning, while Alasdair shook his head and made annoyed little puffing noises.

No one noticed when she stood up and stretched. And no one noticed when she lowered herself down through the trapdoor. It was getting dark in the stairwell. She looked about nervously into the darkness and backed up to the wall. A couple of stabs at her phone, and the flashlight app glowed. That was better—now she could see. Down the stairs, back against the wall she went, holding the glowing phone at arm's length like a protective talisman. She rattled the doors—nothing doing there—and made her cautious way down to the bottom.

Gah, the stink hadn't gone away.

Nothing down here. Only the door that she knew was locked and the stupid fireplace thing, and what was the use of that without a chimney?

What is *the use of that*, she thought.

Careful not to step on any of the gross stuff on the floor, she made her way over to the big, stone structure. It was set deeply into the wall, and her glowing phone made some strange shadows on one side. On a whim, she stuck her head inside and found she could stand upright. Weird. Where there should have been a solid stone wall there was a little gap, a passage that seemed to go back into the wall and . . . down.

"Now tell me again why we're doing this?"

"Will you stop your whining, Alasdair?" snapped Terry. "It was either explore Sandra's secret passage, or freeze to death up on the roof. And who locked us in here in the first place?"

"Yeah. Thanks for the reminder. I'd nearly forgotten."

They had squeezed through the opening in the fireplace (Dave had done a lot of the squeezing), and had found themselves in an inverted V-shaped passage. The walls of rock might have came together thirty feet above their heads, but even with the combined power of three cell phones it was hard to see the top.

"Natural cleavage plane," offered Sandra, who was in the rear.

"Cleavage?" sniggered Alasdair.

"Place where two rock formations come together," she said. "Prob'ly come out at the beach. Looks stable. Prob'ly not dangerous. I've been in plenty of caves like this in the Sierra Nevada. Spelunking, y'know, at the midterm break."

The floor was slippery and irregular, and Terry took the lead. She had knotted her sheet in a couple of places and pulled it up in front to create

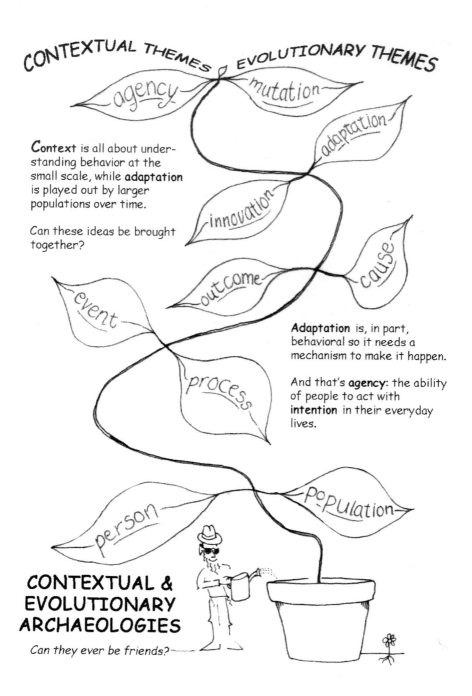

CONTEXTUAL THEMES ⚬ EVOLUTIONARY THEMES

agency   mutation

adaptation

Context is all about understanding behavior at the
small scale, while **adaptation**
is played out by larger
populations over time.

innovation

Can these ideas be brought
together?

cause

event   outcome

Adaptation is, in part,
behavioral so it needs a
mechanism to make it happen.

And that's **agency**: the ability
of people to act with
intention in their everyday
lives.

process

person   population

CONTEXTUAL &
EVOLUTIONARY
ARCHAEOLOGIES

Can they ever be friends?

a droopy diaper effect. At least it was stable. Sandra's analysis of the geology was right, it seemed. The passage continued relatively straight. It was clearly a natural feature and led . . . somewhere. She went slowly, carefully, for although the walls reflected the light it was hard to see more than a couple of feet ahead, and a sprained ankle would mess everything up. The air was damp and still. There was not a sound, apart from the crunching of their steps. After a few minutes they rested on a large rock. The silence was awesome, broken only by their breathing.

They grinned at each other. This was quite an adventure.

After a few minutes' more trekking, the group came to a cave-in and had to climb over a low mound.

"Careful of these shale rocks," said Terry over her shoulder. "They slide all over the place."

But once over the top, she realized that this was only the toe of big collapse. The passage was sealed almost to the top.

"Well, I suppose that's the end of our little adventure," said Terry. "The rocks on this side are too big to move. And no way Dave could fit through that gap."

"But I can." Sandra clambered up the side and slipped through the opening. "I can clear it from this side," she yelled from the other side.

"Yeah, exercise some agency, why don't ya," said Alasdair, sitting on a rock.

There was silence from the other side of the opening.

"Sandra, are you OK?"

"Yes. Be quiet," she shushed, and all was still.

Alasdair exhaled noisily. "Well, what is it? Monsters?"

"I can hear something. It sounds like . . . people talking."

CHAPTER TEN
"P" IS FOR POSTMODERN

In Which a Postmodern Kind of Truth Is Told

"Well? What are they saying?" snapped Alasdair.

"Can't tell." Sandra stopped throwing rocks from the blockage into the passage behind her. She scrambled down the slope and took a few steps toward the noise. "Too dark to get closer," she said. "The voices are kinda garbled. Can't make any sense out of it."

"Prob'ly a bunch of postmodern theorists."

Terry laughed. "Good one, Alasdair."

"Thank you so much. At least one can tell what Marxists like you actually think, however absurd it is. In my humble opinion, old Dave here is so quiet because postmodernists don't know *what* they think."

The turned to the big man, who was grunting in his effort to shift the oversized rocks. He dragged a sleeve over his forehead and flopped down. Terry punched him playfully on the arm.

"Come on, Dave. Give us the official po-mo position on the Neolithic."

"Be happy to. 'Cept that the whole point of postmodernism is that there's no official position on anything."

"Er, did I miss something? How can you have, like, a theoretical orientation that has no position?" Sandra's voice echoed from the far side of the rock pile.

"A naive but oddly perceptive question, Sandy," sneered Alasdair, whose mood seemed to be settling lower with their drop in elevation. "Well, how about it, big guy?"

"I don't want to bore you with the details," began Dave.

"Too late," said Alasdair under his breath.

"What?"

"I said it's late. Just get on with it, Dave."

The large one looked around sheepishly and took a hit from his flask. "Not sure where to start," he mumbled. "Although a good place would be to set Alasdair straight on the difference between **postprocessualism** and postmodernism."

"So kind of you to help," said Alasdair coldly.

"I'm sure you'll find some opportunity to reciprocate." Dave stroked the day-old whiskers on his Neanderthal jaw and addressed himself to Sandra through the widening hole.

"You remember that the New Archeologists were interested in finding out what cultural, social, or ecological processes are behind human history. Basically, they looked at culture as the way people adapt to their environment. Of course, this view hasn't gone away over time, 'cause it's a useful way of looking at things. But as time went on, more and more of them felt that all this emphasis on forces and processes was leaving something out of the equation."

"Like people?" shouted Sandra through the hole.

"Yep. They felt that archaeology had gotten so bound up in behavioral models and quantification that the people themselves had sort of faded into insignificance. According to the models that the processualists were using, people didn't seem to have much of a role in making their own futures. From what they wrote, it was all a matter of forces acting on each other. Now, no one's saying that people are free agents who create societies and cultures without regard to the actual conditions in the real world. But the new generation said that history involves real people making actual decisions. They're called postprocessualists because they, like, came after the New Archeologists and their processualism.

"The Marxists and that lot had been saying this for years. And they sort of joined forces with other folks who used nonprocessual approaches like structuralism and feminism to create a bunch of alternatives to the orthodoxy of processual archaeology. So what it comes down to is that there are lots of approaches that could get labeled 'postprocessual' simply 'cause they reject processualism."

"How does this postmodern thing fit in?" echoed Sandra's voice. "And talk louder. I can't hear."

ACADEMIC SMACKDOWN!!

THE EMPIRICAL, MODERNIST ARCHAEOLOGISTS
They don't believe nothing they can't count!

vs.

THE INCOMPREHENSIBLE, FRENCH, PO-MO PHILOSOPHERS
So obtuse that they can't even understand each other!

Meshuggener mush-brain!

Colonialist lacky!

Science hater!

Dopey empiricist!

Intellectually lazy!

Sloppy scholarship!

THE MODERNISTS...

REALITY exists. It's independent of our conceptualizations of it

THERE are objective facts & we can know them

THINGS have definite meanings

PROOF comes from scientific endeavor

FIXED canon guides research

ACADEMIC study

BEHAVIOR is patterned

DISTANCE from subject is desired

ETHNOGRAPHY is the product

ANALYSIS reveals structure

THE POSTMODERNISTS...

REALITY is a construct. It's a function of how we conceptualize it

ALL knowledge is relative

THERE are endless interpretations

PROOF is a fallacy, an illusion

DIVERSE approaches to research

PRAXIS

BEHAVIOR is variable

PARTICIPATION with subject is mandatory

DECONSTRUCTION is the goal

ANALYSIS reveals writer's presuppositions

‹End of theory joke›

‹Theory joke begins›

So these two archaeologists walk into a bar.

"I published my book with a $10,000 grant from the National Science Foundation," says the first. "Yeah, I know," says the other. "I just got $12,000 from the National Endowment for the Arts to deconstruct it!"

Q. How many neo-Marxist archaeologists does it take to change a light bulb?
A. None. Every light bulb contains the seeds of it's own revolution.

Q. How many postmodern archaeologists does it take to change a light bulb?
A. I reject the notion that it has to be "changed." Rather, the bulb site palimpsest should be added to by the "replacement" element, thereby encouraging subaltern interpretations of "whiteness" and "darkness." See my article in the most recent Current Anthropology.

‹Joke ends here due to lack of space.›

Alasdair and Terry groaned in unison.

"That's a long story," went on Dave. "And I hope we'll be out of here before I can finish. But I'll tell you how it relates to one postprocessual approach. It's called *contextual* or *interpretive* archaeology. Although no one seems to want to saddle it with a permanent tag. People who take this approach don't like the idea that you can account for what happened in the past—or the present, for that matter—by a single theory. Economic, environmental, psychological, or whatever. In fact, they tend to think these metatheories just box us in and make us think in one dimension about the things we dig up. Interpretive archaeologists say that artifacts have no fixed meaning that we can discover. They say the meaning of an artifact to the people who used it depended on the context in which it was used."

"Like Jim Deetz's example of the candle," chipped in Sandra, pleased that she could contribute. "A candle's, like, a utilitarian object when we use it to light a dark corner. Or a romantic symbol if you put a couple on the dinner table. Or a religious object during a Catholic Mass."

"Right. So we can never really understand what an artifact means without first knowing the context it was used in. Interpretive archaeologists say that artifacts are like texts: you can either understand them literally or as metaphor. And in the same way that artifacts don't have fixed meanings, there's no one single past out there to be known. The critical theorists and the feminists and the rest have their perspectives, but none can claim to explain it. All they can do is interpret it."

"Now just a minute, big guy," interrupted Alasdair. "If artifacts and sites are texts that have a variety of meanings, then how can we ever know what happened in the past?"

"We can't. At least not in the way you mean it, since there was no one past to know."

"If I thought that was true, I'd give up archaeology as a waste of time."

"And a thousand archy sites sigh with relief," put in Terry. "But for once, and probably the last time this decade, I agree with you. This contextual approach or whatever you call it is an intellectual dead end. In fact, it's a step backward."

"Quite so," interrupted Alasdair. "In my humble opinion, the whole approach is hopelessly relativistic. If there's no actual past, no facts, and no understandable meanings out there, then how do we decide what's a reasonable approach to take to understand the past? If everyone has a seat at the table, are you going to set a place for that nut Erich von Däniken, who thinks extraterrestrials built the pyramids, as well as for Dr. Tuliver? And what about the Children of Odin? Just because *they* believe their imaginary gods have sent them out here to rebury the skeleton we dug up, does it mean we have to hand it over?"

Not waiting for Dave to defend himself, Terry jumped into the argument.

"Alasdair's right. Relativism is a dead end. If you say that the past is up for grabs, you totally trivialize the great themes that run through human history—like the class struggle—by giving equal weight to every flaky idea from the front page of the frikkin' *National Enquirer*. I don't know if archaeology's a science or not. But we have to give our research agenda some priorities. Otherwise the field'll disintegrate into a million particularistic studies with no connection with each other."

Dave nodded somberly. At first, the half pint of vodka had loosened him up, but now it was starting to slow him down.

"Yeah. I'm not saying you're wrong. There's some danger of that, I suppose. But think of the alternative. We don't write history with Europe at its center anymore, 'cause we recognize it's ethnocentric. Well, in the same way, I can't see throwing interpretive models out of the window 'cause they're not part of the accepted intellectual tradition. You're right that the view we end up with isn't as coherent and comforting as your cut-and-dried social science models. But it's certainly more interesting. And more like real human life."

"Ach! They're off having a party with Manuel and my crew, I bet," said Hans, casually taking another bread roll from the platter. "You know how the kids are." He ripped the roll in half, slathered it with enough butter to clog a minor artery, and looked around the dining-room table for more.

Ian Tuliver, whose own concept of a healthy diet consisted of eating the pickle on his hamburger, gave the photographer a look of contempt. "But where *are* they, Mr. Wurst? You say that you arranged to meet them, and they didn't show up."

"Ja. Something like that." A fair portion of a chicken leg disappeared into Hans's mouth.

"Then where *are* they?" repeated Tuliver. He looked at Ollie Bott for support, but the excavation's patron was hidden behind a newspaper, his feet up on the couch.

Hans shrugged.

"Got lost, maybe. If you're so concerned, you look for them, Herr Tulifer."

"I dispatched Dr. Green to search an hour ago. She knows the area surprisingly well, and it would do no good for me to go blundering about in the dark."

"Ah, sure. The Green and the old woman. They find 'em all right."

"Old woman? What old woman was that?" Bott spoke from behind his newspaper, and there was a tone in his voice that might have been anxiety.

"I donno. Some old woman in the big hat. They walking together down that path toward the ocean."

"Talking?"

"Sure talking. What else would they be doing?"

The newspaper was down now, and Bott's uneasiness showed in his face.

"Mr. Bott," said Tuliver impatiently, "I fail to see that this has any relevance to the task at hand. I am personally responsible for the safety of these students, and . . ."

"Keep your pants on, Tuliver. You're becoming a real pain in the behind."

"This is intolerable," sputtered Tuliver, jumping up from his chair. "I don't have to come here to be insulted."

"Ja?" asked Hans, shaking his mangled chicken femur at the professor. "Where you usually go then? Huh? Ha! Ha!"

Tuliver snatched up his briefcase and threw a hateful look at Bott. The Austrian was clearly insane, and Bott was worse. The man had no conception of science and was capable of anything. Tuliver massaged his temples and breathed hard. He should never have become involved in this train wreck of a project, and it was time to pull out. To hell with the site and the whole mad crowd of them.

Someone or other once claimed that it's always darkest before the dawn. Not so in the case of Ian Nigel Tuliver. For him, the worst was yet to come.

There was a scraping sound, and the old boxlike TV that sat in front of the fireplace began to shudder. It jerked forward a foot, and a pile of papers that had accumulated on top of it fell to the floor.

"Earthquake!" squeaked Tuliver. He stood quivering like a codfish with his mouth open.

Bott jumped to his feet.

"What the . . . ?" And the TV stopped its perambulations.

With Terry in the lead, the four adventurers emerged from the false side of the fireplace. The anachronisms of their pseudo-Neolithic garb had been softened in the lantern light but now were exposed in the glare of the bare electric bulb. They were hungry and cold, but very relieved to find that the subterranean passage led somewhere.

"What's this? A costume party?" snapped Tuliver, looking his students up and down. "Where the hell have you come from?" He didn't wait for an explanation. "You have inconvenienced Mr. Wurst, Dr. Green, and myself by your unprofessional behavior. And now . . . were you hiding in there? Is this a joke?"

Terry elbowed Alasdair in the ribs. "I told you Dr. Tuliver didn't know about the costumes. And *he* was the one who didn't show up." Terry tried to simultaneously hold her robe together and point at Hans. "If we hadn't found that underground passage, we'd still be stuck in the frikkin' tower."

As the grimy group dumped themselves onto chairs and couches, the door creaked open. An elderly lady who carried a broad-brimmed hat and had Hannah on her arm took a position on the couch next to Ollie. For once, he seemed speechless. Then two others crept in.

"And what are *they* doing here?" demanded Tuliver, pointing to Sean and Freya, who hovered at the door. "This is a madhouse. Costumed players trapped in towers with Druidic princesses. Whatever next?" Evidently, the lovers had bridged the ethnic divide that had briefly separated them, for they stood hand in hand.

"They're here because they have *information* that concerns you and you." Hannah nodded firmly at Tuliver and Ollie Bott in turn.

"Have you been asleep for the past week, Green?" groaned Tuliver in frustration. "She is one of the despicable group who made off with the skeleton."

"Are you sure of that?" said Hannah mysteriously. "Did you ever wonder how they got to hear of the remains, when only the archaeological crew knew about them?"

All eyes turned to Freya, who tossed her hair and said quite simply, "Someone left a message on the altar where we do . . . er . . . did our afternoon ceremonies. All it said was that the archaeologists had dug up the bones of a European. That's all. So we went on over."

"Oh, very likely," scoffed Tuliver. "And it was signed 'A Friend,' am I right? I blame the Internet for the present generation's failure to distinguish reality from fiction."

"Matter of fact, it was signed 'A Friend.' And I know what I saw," said Freya stiffly.

"Then it was that . . . that viper." Tuliver indicated Sean with the smallest inclination of his head. "He must have slunk off surreptitiously and left the note."

Terry spoke up. "Nope. He was working with me the whole time."

"Then who done it?" spluttered Tuliver.

"Did it," corrected Hannah. "Whom did you tell, Ian?"

"Only Mr. Bott here." He indicated Ollie, who had been very quiet since the group's arrival. "Surely you're not suggesting that he had anything to do with it? You have completely lost your senses, Green. This does not bode well for tenure, you know."

Hannah ignored the threat. She turned to Alice Bott, who was smiling angelically at nothing in particular.

"Miss Bott, you grew up here on Dougal's Island, didn't you? Do you remember how things used to be here in the old days?"

"Oh yes," said the old woman, fingering her oversize hat. "Occasionally I find myself forgetting things that happened yesterday, but my girlhood's as clear as crystal. Strange how that happens, isn't it, dear? I must be getting old." Miss Bott faded off into silence and was gently put back on track by Hannah.

"I was in one of the last classes here," she gestured around vaguely. "I graduated in '32 with Milly Stewart, Bettina and Marina Shannon, Victoria Fine, Violet Huff, and Dotty McInnes. They're all gone now, except for Dotty. Never did care much for Dotty. And after that, I stayed on to help Mother with the younger girls. Teaching ancient history and such. Mother was very keen on ancient history, you know. Particularly British history. Her family was from England, you know. Somewhere out in the

West Country, where they have all those marvelous megalithic monuments. Marvelous megalithic monuments," she said again, savoring the mellifluous sound of the phrase, and she drifted off into a reverie once more.

"Miss Bott? What were you telling me about the ceremonies at the mound?" asked Hannah softly.

Freya looked up with interest and gripped Sean's hand.

"Oh, yes. Mother was a strong believer in the Old Religion. I think she thought of herself as a priestess," said Miss Bott confidentially. "On special nights, the equinoxes and such, all we girls would dress up in our robes and make offerings to the carving of the Great Goddess. Ah, the memories. When I saw those young girls today, all dressed up and looking so pretty"—she smiled kindly at Terry—"it brought it all back. Milly, Bettina, and me."

"And when your mother passed away? Do you remember that?"

"Oh yes, dear. But it was such a long time ago. She wanted to be buried here on the island. I was quite young at the time, and pretty, too. Though you would hardly know it now." She paused, fishing for a compliment, with which Hannah obliged.

"And she was buried . . . ?"

"In the old way, just as she asked. Didn't I just tell you this, dear?"

"What do you mean, Miss Bott, 'in the old way'?"

"Oh, like the ancient women of the deep past. In her stone crypt out under her mound."

"What?" Tuliver popped out of his chair as if he had sat on a bee. "Are you claiming that the skeleton I . . . we uncovered is only sixty years old? I won't believe it! And besides, it's gone, so there's no evidence."

"Except for the bone sample that I sent off with my friend bd starr for radiocarbon dating," added Hannah. "I imagine that will clear up any ambiguity."

"But the mound itself and the carving," said Tuliver, desperately clinging to the arms of his chair. "Surely they are authentic."

"Oh yes, dear," smiled Miss Bott. "Entirely authentic."

Tuliver sighed with relief and flopped back into his seat.

"Mother herself cut the picture of the Great Goddess from the *International Geographic* and had it carved by Miss Whitmore, our sculpture teacher. She was a niece of Sir Henry Whitmore, who was commissioned by Prince Albert himself for a portrait. Perhaps you've heard of him?"

Stifling a laugh, Hans Wurst emitted a kind of snort.

"And the mound?" groaned Tuliver, careless of Sir Henry's illustrious career.

"Accurate down to the smallest detail," smiled Miss Bott luminously. "A perfect copy of Oldgrange Barrow in the English West Country. Have you found the passage in your diggings, Professor Toliphant? I recall we had a tea party there in the spring of '24, before the laborers filled it over. It was a glorious year, you know. Happy days and moonlight picnics on the beach with Mother. All gone now," said the old lady dreamily. "Past and gone."

At this, Hans's laughter overwhelmed his ability to restrain it, and he began to roar, pounding the floor with his heavy boots.

"That's a great joke. Even better than mine. The great discovery, mound, carving, body. All as phony as . . . as them rented costumes." The crew moved uncomfortably in their seats, and Sandra folded her arms across her tightly laced bodice.

But Hannah shook her head. "Not quite all. The skeleton was real enough, as was the pottery. I guess, Mr. Bott, that you took the remains of your grandmother to keep this game going a little longer. For I'm sure you realized that any experienced archaeologist could tell a modern skeleton from an ancient one just by looking at it." Tuliver winced. "And that would put a stop to everything. But I *would* like to know about the pottery."

Ollie Bott had sat quietly to this point, showing neither surprise nor anger at the accusations. Now, he cocked his head to one side and smiled at her.

"Well, well. I took you for one smart lady straight off, Doc. And so you turned out to be. Figured out my little game from end to end, you did." He made a half turn toward his aunt. "And don't you worry about your mama, Miss Alice. She's planted in a real nice place out overlooking the bay. She'd like that, she would."

Although Alice Bott smiled and nodded at the mention of her name, Hannah thought it unlikely she comprehended what had become of her mother's bones.

"And the pottery sherds? Why, they were easiest of all. I just paid cash for a big ole bag through some treasure-hunting magazine and scattered 'em around up there. Glad to hear they were real. Guess I got my money's worth."

"Which would explain why the diggers found them only on the surface and not in the mound itself," said Hannah.

"But it was an understandable error. Surely you can see that," pleaded Tuliver to the company. A vision of massive humiliation flashed through his brain. Would any of his colleagues ever take him seriously again?

Tuliver's thoughts were transparent to Hannah, and she let that question hang out there for a few moments before continuing.

"OK," she continued. "So now we understand how you pulled off this prank, but not why you did it. What could your motive possibly be?"

"Prank? You call this a prank, Green?" blustered Tuliver. "It's a hoax, a disgraceful fraud. And the perpetrator shall be prosecuted to the fullest extent of the law."

Bott leaned back and put his western boots up on a chair in a display of nonchalance.

"Now, now. Prosecuted, Tuliver? For what? For scattering some old pieces of pottery on my land? For giving a dumb-ass professor and his crew free room and board? Guess I should have told the county coroner that we was going to rebury my own grandmother's remains on my property. I'll mention it to him at our next Rotary Club meeting."

He yawned extravagantly and leaned back farther still, hands clasped behind his neck. "It's been a good run, Tuliver. But now our friend from the *Geographic* has his pictures, it's time for you all to leave."

Tuliver's mouth dropped open, and a jumble of questioning sounds emerged.

"Wha . . . wha . . . ? I mean . . . Wha . . . ?"

Ollie turned toward Hans, and they chuckled conspiratorially.

"This professor ain't so smart, I don't think," said the photographer, spinning a large finger by the side of his head in the international symbol for mental confusion. "How about the lady doctor, does she get it?"

"Oh yes, she gets it," said Hannah. The truth was now clear to her: that she and Tuliver had been manipulated for the second oldest motive of all—money. "And she also has enough German to know *Hans Wurst* means a joker. This is all about notoriety, isn't it? About getting publicity for this healthing spa, or whatever you're going to call it."

"I call it a retreat center. But, y'know, "healthing spa" sounds even better. Mind if we use it?"

Ignoring this impertinent remark, Hannah went on for Tuliver's benefit. The man was arrogant, mean-spirited, and malicious, but he had been used and abused, and his fragile ego had taken quite a blow.

"This is how I see it, Ian. Here's Mr. Bott stuck out here on an island in the middle of nowhere. His only assets are a hotel-size building and a pseudo-Neolithic site built by an eccentric relative. He knows about the recent interest in Native American religion—possibly from an introductory anthropology class—and puts all the elements together: he'll make Dougal's Island a destination on the New Age ritual tour circuit, to compete with Sedona, Arizona, and Glastonbury in England, and the rest. He has this vision of goddess worshipers, seekers of power convergences, and other pilgrims flocking here. And staying at his hotel. Perhaps he'll put up a gift shop and sell pendants in the shape of the Dougal's Island Venus."

"Another good idea. Thanks, Doc."

"But first he needs to legitimize the site. And that's where the archaeologists come in. After all, who has more authority than a university professor? If Dr. Tuliver says it's authentic, who's going to argue? And if he could get a popular magazine to publicize it for him, so much the better. Well, Mr. Bott, you've won the game. I dare say Hans's photographs will get published somewhere. Though I don't suppose *International Geographic* will take them."

"You're right there, Doc." The photographer's accent had gone the way of his cover story. "No, the folks at the *Geographic* won't be interested in the story of a gullible professor. Nothing unusual about that. But there's a whole raft of other mags that'll take it. I think Dr. Tuliver can look for his portrait in *Oracle*, *Earth Time*, and *Power Circles*."

"And don't forget *National Investigator*," added Hannah softly. She was enjoying this. "Congratulations, Ian. You're going to be famous, after all."

EPILOGUE

In Which Everyone Gets Just What They Get

I f this tale were pure fiction, your author might have introduced some deus ex machina to ensure that evil was punished and that the virtuous received their just rewards. (Several scenarios have, in fact, just flashed into his head.) However, for better or worse, this tale is about the practice of archaeology. And no one but the severely myopic could confuse that with the so-called real world.

Thus, we are left with the kind of morally equivocal ending that will no doubt be abhorrent to television evangelists and others with little tolerance for ambiguity of any sort.

- They are the kind of people who would appreciate neither this book nor its message.

- They are the kind of people who expect science to provide all the answers and feel let down and fearful when it doesn't.

- They get from archaeology as much as they are willing to give. Expecting and accepting only hard answers phrased as facts, they ask questions that can be answered in these terms.

And that, I suppose, is OK for them.

But you, oh wise and perceptive reader, can see further.

You have concluded (as Sean suggested in chapter 1) that archaeologists can do no more than tell stories about the past. Some are stories of harmony, others of discord. Some pass the test of Occam's razor, others don't. Some sound plausible but have no data to back them up.

An eminent archaeologist of an earlier era once used the onion analogy to describe the process of doing archaeology. Archaeologists strip away the layers, he wrote, and find the truth at the center.

Sounds profound, but it's misleading because—in the opinion of your author—it presupposes that there is a *single truth* out there to be found. A better analogy, although without any gustatory appeal, might be one of those pictures made up of thousands of multicolored dots. If you look at the picture through a red lens, you see one image, with a blue lens a different image, and so on. Theoretical models are like these colored lenses, for they help us see patterns in the archaeological record that would otherwise be invisible. Different lenses are useful for seeing the various elements of the image. None shows all of them, and it is up to the observer to decide which image is the most revealing for his or her purpose.

The archaeological record contains many levels of meaning. On the surface level, what biblical scholars call **p'shat**, we can discover the dates and designs of things. Who did what and where. That much is easy and needs techniques, not theories.

But to dig below the surface (so to speak), to speculate about *why* people did what they did—either consciously, or as unknowing participants in a never-ending historical/political/ecological process—*that* requires a tolerance for ambiguity. It also helps to have some humility, to recognize that today's stunning insights may tomorrow be no more than orange peels on the compost pile of intellectual history.

Returning to this manuscript after a hiatus, your author feels it his duty to bring the long-suffering reader up to date on the fates of our characters.

IAN TULIVER, Ph.D., RPA, F.R.S.A., received a complimentary write-up in *Power Circles* magazine and has recently accepted the position of Dean of the School of Psychic Archaeology at the University of Invercargill, New Zealand. He serves as editor-in-chief of the *Journal of Really Neat Old Stuff*.

Dr Tuliver accepts the deanship.

Another hard day at the office for Hannah.

HANNAH GREEN is currently interim Director of Antiquities for the new Palestinian State. An enthusiastic sportswoman—she placed eighteenth in a recent Jerusalem Marathon—Hannah also enjoys whitewater rafting on the river Jordan, and is an occasional contributor to *International Geographic*.

SEAN DOYLE is Assistant Manager of the New Magik Healthing Spa and Retreat Centre. **FREYA** and he are raising their twins in the mainstream Wiccan tradition.

And they lived happily ever after.

FINIS

TALKING POINTS

Use the theoretical discussions engaged in by our protagonists as jumping-off points, places to begin the journey of teasing out meaning and separating mere opinion from reasoned conclusions. Remember, it's more important to start out in archaeology by getting an understanding of its *logic* than by memorizing who invaded whom and which culture's pots have that squiggly line around the top. At least, that's my reasoned conclusion.

Some folks who don't have much of a background in archaeology may have to do some research before they can deal with these questions. So get to it.

Chapter 1

What is science? Are the social sciences so different in method from the hard sciences like chemistry? Who decides which research questions are *worth* pursuing?

What did Hannah mean when she said that she liked to think of herself as using "the scientific method to approach questions that are essentially humanistic"?

Chapter 2

What is Cultural Resources Management, and how different is it from archaeology? Is Occam's razor a useful principle? What are its limits? Is it wrong for scientists to falsify their results? Why? Thinking of Claude's rocks, is there a point where one should draw a line, as far as open-mindedness is concerned, or is everything just a "matter of opinion"?

Do you, like Sean, believe in love at first sight? (Be honest, now.) Is *that* a matter of opinion?

Chapter 3

Why were the archaeologists of the early twentieth century primarily interested in reconstructing history? What's meant by a *historical* explanation of events?

Chapter 4

The New Archeologists used to say that "archeology is anthropology or it is nothing." What did they mean by that? Histories of archaeology make a big deal about the rise of the New Archeology. Was it really *that* important? Can one really make valid, specieswide generalizations about human behavior? Assuming that you could, why would you *want* to do such a thing?

What do you think about the idea that culture is the way that societies adapt to their various environments? Which aspects of modern Western culture does this concept explain?

Chapter 5

How does the process of diffusion work? Can you think of any contemporary examples? (And "no" is not an acceptable response, thank you.) What's the connection between a community's social structure and its ability to create massive pieces of architecture? Put another way, could a band society have built the Egyptian pyramids? What happens to egalitarianism as societies get bigger?

State societies are bigger than bands or chiefdoms and more rationally organized, and they create far more technologically complex stuff (like computers). Does that mean that state societies are *better* than bands? Is "better" a useful concept here?

Chapter 6

What are the limits of cultural relativity? Why would a scientist want to make up categories for things, when cultures have their own groupings already? What's the difference between a materialist and a culturalist explanation? Which is correct? (OK, that was a trick question.) Terry insisted that no one should have the right to restrict scholars' access to information about the past. Do you agree?

Sometimes the government forcibly takes private land for some overriding public benefit. Is there a point where private property rights end and the national interest in documenting the past begins? Should Native Americans and other First Nation peoples get to decide what happens to the remains of people they consider to be their ancestors? What if that means that scientists never find out how our species evolved and settled the earth?

Chapter 7

Is there *really* much of a difference between sex and gender? Is feminist archaeology politics, science, or something else? Do feminist archaeologists have to be women? How could archaeological interpretations affect contemporary attitudes toward gender roles? (You're reading this book, aren't you?)

Chapter 8

Archaeologists come up with research questions for their sites that they think will shed light on the *big* issues, like the processes that held societies together and those that pulled them apart. That's why there's so much interest in Karl Marx's model of history. Why was Marx so keen on revolution?

What's the connection between Marx's kind of materialism and that of the functionalists? If optimal foraging theory helps us understand how people use their natural environment, why would a Marxist-influenced archaeologist object to the approach? Why are Marxist-influenced archaeologists interested in ideology?

Chapter 9

If you reject the idea of Progress and the idea that some societies are "better" than others, does that mean all cultures are equally good? How about all cultural practices: are they all OK? How would you measure "progress"? (Oh, oh. Looks like we've wandered back to Culturalrelativity-land.)

Do people really have agency, or is it just a feel-good idea that lets us think we have some control? How does structuration help us understand the tension between the personal agency we'd like to have and the structures of everyday life (what Pierre Bourdieu calls *habitus*) that we live in?

Why isn't neoevolutionism just another determinist approach . . . or is it? If adaptation doesn't always make things more complex, why not just say "change" instead of "evolution"? (OK, that's a trick question.)

Chapter 10

How are Marxist and feminist archaeologies "postprocessual"? Come to think of it, what is *processual* archaeology? Why do archaeologists insist that artifacts have no fixed meanings? If this is true, how are we to interpret archaeological sites?

To what degree is there a *real*, objective past out there for archaeologists to discover? Why not use Wikipedia as your only source for an essay if you say you're a postmodernist? Are scholarship and scholarly knowledge (like universities and this book) arbitrary elements of *habitus*? Do you believe that these ideas are useful to help understand the world . . . or are you just going along for the ride?

GLOSSARY

agency The idea that people actively and intentionally shape their world. In archaeology, it emerged as a reaction to theories that emphasize big, impersonal cultural and environmental processes. (*See also* Determinism.)

anthropology The holistic study of humankind from biological, social, and cultural perspectives.

archaeological record, the Artifacts, layers of soil, structural remains, and everything else that one finds on an archaeological site that, put together, enables us to reconstruct past human behavior.

archaeology (1) The study of past human behavior based on material remains. (2) "The most fun you can have with your pants on" (Kent Flannery). (*See also* New Archeology.)

artifact Anything made or modified by people: this book, a 100,000-year-old spear point, or my former 1968 VW van.

Aztec The last of a series of Central American civilizations that flourished until the Spanish invasion of 1519. For five hundred years, the Aztec people created cities with massive civil and religious buildings, developed intensive agriculture, and controlled an extensive empire. (*See also* State.)

band A term used by anthropologists to denote small societies of mobile, egalitarian hunter-gatherer peoples. Bands have the simplest known social structure. (*See also* Service, Elman.)

Binford, Lewis A founding father of the *New Archeology* movement. His 1962 article "Archeology as Anthropology" (*American Antiquity* 28:217–25) inspired a generation of archaeologists, mostly in North America, to strive for greater methodological rigor and to commit themselves to the creation of an anthropology of the past. One of the great ones.

boychik (Yiddish) Affectionate term for a young man.

Çatalhöyük An 8,000-year-old Neolithic town in central Anatolia, Turkey.

chiefdom A term used by anthropologists to denote societies organized on the basis of rank—that is, people are born into their places in society. Chiefdoms are generally governed by a hereditary ruler. In contrast to *bands*, they are far from egalitarian. (*See also* Service, Elman.)

Childe, V. Gordon An Australian-born archaeologist known for interpretations of European and Near Eastern prehistory that emphasized the role of class conflict in the creation of history. If that sounds like the philosophy of *Karl Marx*, you're right. Childe's 1936 book *Man Makes Himself* is well worth reading.

CRM Cultural resources management. The practice of protecting and managing archaeological sites and other important cultural properties through public policy and a conservation ethic.

cultural diffusion The observation that ideas, technologies, and artifacts can move from one place to another, from one culture to another.

cultural ecology The study of human culture as a mechanism by which societies adapt to their varied natural environments.

cultural relativity The position that no culture is intrinsically "better" than any other. Modern British society, for example, is not superior to that of Australian Aborigines, it's just different. This idea developed in response to ethnocentric Victorian scientists who liked to rank the world's cultures, invariably putting themselves on the top of a heap of dark-skinned others. (*See also* Progress.)

culture process The underlying "why" of culture. Cultural process was the watchword, the Holy Grail, for practitioners of the *New Archeology* who were interested in the relationship between the social, environmental, and economic forces that drive society.

determinism The idea that specific, identifiable factors "determine" the direction of culture and history. Environmental determinism, for example, holds that culture is largely an outcome of humans' adaptations to their natural environment: thus, environment "determines" culture.

digbum (*See* Shovelbum.)

emic/etic Categories devised by participants in a culture versus those imposed by the scientific observer.

empiricist One who believes only what can be directly observed.

epistemology The study of how we know what we think we know.

ethnoarchaeology The study of the cultural practices of contemporary peoples for clues by which to understand the archaeological record.

feminist archaeology An approach that places women at the center of archaeological analysis to restore gender balance to the history of "man." (After Joan Gero.)

functionalism A theoretical approach that emphasizes the adaptive function of cultural traits. Functionalism sees an analogy between the elements of a given culture and the organs of a living creature. In both cases, it is claimed, the parts work together to ensure the survival of the whole.

gender Social categories, such as "gentleman" and "lady," that are full of cultural expectations of the people we put into them. A person's role in society has more to do with his or her socially defined gender than with his or her biological sex.

Gimbutas, Marija An archaeologist and art historian who proposed that Neolithic societies in southeastern Europe were peaceful, matrifocal, and goddess-worshiping. Although her 1982 book *The Goddess and Gods of Old Europe* does not have much support among archaeologists, Gimbutas's work is heavily cited by followers of the Goddess movement.

Grimes Graves Deep, extensive Neolithic-era flint mine in central England.

Hodder, Ian A British archaeologist, an excavator known as one of the chief proponents of a *postmodern* archaeology. His 1999 book *The Archaeological Process* isn't light reading, but is well worth the effort.

hunter-gatherer/forager Peoples who make their living by . . . ah . . . hunting and gathering. Hunter-gatherers live in simple *band* societies now—and presumably way back into the *Paleolithic*.

indigenous invention The idea that a particular group's culture developed by its own independent invention rather than by contact with other peoples.

Kennewick Man (aka the Ancient One) A nine-thousand-year-old skeleton found near Kennewick, Washington. While local Native Americans claimed the remains as an ancestor and wished to rebury them, a group of scientists filed suit to study what they believed was a unique archaeological discovery that could add to our knowledge of the peopling of North America. A matter of "your data is my grandmother."

Kenyon, Kathleen A pioneer of stratigraphic archaeological excavation in the Near East, notably at Jericho, during the 1950s.

mamser (Yiddish) Bastard. In most languages, an insult that has nothing to do with parentage.

Marxism Karl Marx was a nineteenth-century German philosopher, historian, sociologist, and revolutionary. With his friend Engels, he developed the idea that human history is driven by conflict between social classes. (*See also* Materialism.)

materialism The idea that the material conditions of life determine how we see the world, rather than the reverse.

middle range theory Ideas that help us link the things that we dig up with the processes that created them. (*See also* Ethnoarchaeology.)

Midwestern Taxonomic System In 1939, the system took a stack of local cultural chronologies and turned them into a single, coherent synthesis that described the historical development of Native American cultures in the American Midwest.

Mohenjo-Daro A fabulous archaeological site on the Indus River in Pakistan that was abandoned about four thousand years ago. The city, whose population was about twenty thousand, is famous for its strict grid plan and very sophisticated drainage and refuse disposal systems. (*See* State.)

National Historic Preservation Act A U.S. law that requires, among other things, that federal agencies "take into account" the effect of their activities on important archaeological sites and other cultural resources. Cynics sometimes call it the "Archaeologists Full Employment Act." (*See also* CRM.)

neoevolutionism A theory of social change based on Darwin's ideas of fitness and adaptation.

Neolithic A period of Old World prehistory characterized by the development of agriculture, which in turn led to the establishment of permanent settlements and complex societies.

New Archeology A movement, involving mostly North American archaeologists, that emphasized using the *scientific method* and quantification to study cultural processes rather than "mere" chronology. I have intentionally left out the second *a* in the word *archeology*, in keeping with the practice of the New Archeologists, who saw it as archaic and a symbol of European hegemony. (*See also* Processual Archaeology and Binford, Lewis.)

Occam's razor A logical principle: the simplest explanation is the most likely to be true.

Paleolithic The period of prehistory that extends from the earliest traces of human culture 2.5 million years ago to about ten thousand years before the present.

poste restante A place to pick up your mail when you have no permanent address.

postmodernism A philosophy that rejects the traditional structure of scientific investigation and scientific authority itself. (*See also* Wikipedia.)

postprocessualism A critical reaction to the functionalism of the *New Archeology*, this movement insists that people have a role in creating their own history and culture. Postprocessual approaches include feminist, neo-Marxist, and contextual archaeologies. (*See* also Processual Archaeology.)

processual archaeology The approach favored by practitioners of the *New Archeology*. (*See also* Culture Process; Materialism; New Archeology; and Scientific Method.)

Progress A still-popular ideology that values change in culture from simple and "primitive" to complex, modern, and generally more like Western society. Nineteenth-century philosophers saw Progress as a Good Thing that should be encouraged. (*See also* Spencer, Herbert.)

provenience The exact place where an artifact is found.

proximate cause The immediate reason something happens, in contrast to underlying, structural causes. The proximate cause of getting soaked is that it's raining. The structural cause may be a ridge of high pressure somewhere up in the atmosphere.

p'shat (Hebrew) The plain meaning of a text, without added interpretation. By analogy, we can extend this approach to imply the simple meanings of artifacts, such as function and chronology.

"Purple Haze" Rock music piece written by Jimi Hendrix and recorded by him in 1967.

radiocarbon dating Devised in 1949, radiocarbon dating enabled archaeologists to work out the exact age of artifacts made of wood, bone, and other organic materials. It revolutionized archaeology.

research design A plan that lays out the investigator's theoretical scheme, research goals, and strategy for getting the project done.

Sandia Cave Prehistoric site in the American Southwest that some suggest was planted with fake artifacts. Your author takes no position on the controversy, fearing the legal implications. Next time you are visiting the dentist, you may care to peruse Douglas Preston's article on the subject in *The New Yorker* (12 June 1995).

scientific method A way of addressing research questions by systematically testing hypotheses using carefully selected data.

segmentary society A term used by anthropologists to denote a basically egalitarian social group that is ordered by kinship. Their settlements are permanent and their economics based on herding or small-scale agriculture. (*See also* Service, Elman.)

Service, Elman An American anthropologist who devised a system to classify societies based on their complexity. (*See also* Band; Segmentary Society; Chiefdom; and State.)

shofar (Hebrew) A ram's-horn trumpet blown at ritually prescribed times.

shovelbum (aka digbum) An itinerant archaeologist who makes his or her living by moving from one archaeological job site to the next. Not such a romantic existence as it sounds.

Spencer, Herbert A nineteenth-century British biologist and philosopher. He came up with the term "survival of the fittest" and applied it as an analogy between nonhuman species and human cultures. Spencer thought that humankind has changed from simple to complex societies as a natural process in which primitive forms are replaced by more adaptive ones. (*See also* Three Ages.)

state A term used by anthropologists to mean a highly complex, populous society administrated by a tax-supported bureaucracy, police force, and legal system. (*See also* Service, Elman.)

structuration "Men make this own history but not under conditions they chose for themselves," wrote *Karl Marx*, but does that mean people have no agency? Structuration deals with the degree to which people both make their own history and are manipulated by structures over which they have no control by rejecting this dualism. As these structures are created and recreated by people conforming to society's rules, structuration is a recursive process that bridges the gap between personal *agency* and *determinism*.

tapu Indigenous system of religious rules, restrictions, and requirements practiced in Hawai'i until 1820.

Taylor, Walter Author of the 1948 classic *A Study of Archeology*. Taylor was frustrated with the descriptive archaeology of the era and called for the field to be reinvented as an integrated study of past cultural adaptations. (*See also* New Archeology.)

teleology The assumption that cultural institutions and practices were made to create observed outcomes—that we can know why something exists by observing what it does.

Three Ages (Stone, Bronze, Iron) A nineteenth-century system that classified ancient societies in supposed evolutionary sequence by means of their technologies. An interesting but incorrect model of the way society works. (*See also* Spencer, Herbert.)

Tikal A city in the Guatemala lowlands built by the Maya civilization about 2,400 years ago. Famous for the rich tombs of its elite ruling class and enormous temple pyramids. (*See also* State.)

von Däniken, Erich Author of *Chariots of the Gods*. This imaginative book suggests that extraterrestrials helped early civilizations build monumental architecture such as the Central American stepped pyramids. (*See also* Wurst, Hans.)

Wikipedia An Internet-based encyclopedia. While traditional scholarly sources are compiled by experts, wiki content can be changed by any user for any reason. Opinion and well-documented research merge in this *postmodern* knowledge base. As a source, it could be a place to start but certainly not to finish your research if you think you're a scholar.

Wurst, Hans The clown or trickster character in German and Yiddish folktales. Literally, "Hans Sausage."

FOR FURTHER READING

For anyone who might still be reading (as well as those who just skipped to the end), I offer the following books, articles, and websites for your edification. These references are not intended to provide a true introduction to the various subjects. Rather, I provide references for the studies mentioned in the text, as well as some of my personal favorites.

For a highly readable introductory survey of archaeological theory by one of the sharpest thinkers around, I still recommend Matthew Johnson's aptly tided *Archaeological Theory: An Introduction* (Oxford: Blackwell, 2010), now in its second edition. If you are cyber-addicted, the United States–based website ArchNet and its European equivalent ARGE are the best sources for things archaeological. Find them at archnet.asu.edu/ and odur.let.rug.nl/arge/tindex.htm, respectively. All the websites were accessed July 2010.

Chapter I. Science and Politics in Archaeology

Professional conferences are great places to observe the behavior of archaeologists in their natural habitat. Registration fees can be high, although students usually get a reduced rate; I would *never* suggest that anyone try to sneak in without paying. Many societies' websites are listed at archnet.asu.edu/institutions/institutions.php. Whether archaeology is a science or not, it certainly can be practiced as a rigorous *social* science. This book's a bit dated and can be heavy going, but it's a classic statement all the same: *Archeological Explanation: The Scientific Method in Archeology*, by Patty Jo Watson, Steven LeBlanc, and Charles Redman (New York: Columbia University Press, 1984). Those interested in methodological

178

rigor in cultural anthropology might delve into *Research Methods in Anthropology: Qualitative and Quantitative Approaches*, by Harvey Bernard (Lanham, Md.: AltaMira Press, 2005). It is one of those rare books that is both scholarly and very readable, and it includes a table of random numbers for the truly committed. Science is all very well, but archaeology has real life-and-death implications in places like Cyprus, Israel, and the former Yugoslavia. For an excellent and very readable account, try *Between Past and Present: Archaeology, Ideology, and Nationalism in the Modern Middle East*, by Neil Asher Silberman (London: Anchor, 1989).

Chapter 2. Cultural Resources Management, Ethics, and Pseudoscience

To find a place on an archaeological excavation in North America, go to the Archaeological Fieldwork server at www.archaeologyfieldwork.com/AFW; this site can also be used, to a limited degree, for other parts of the world. For projects in the United Kingdom, try www.britarch.ac.uk/briefing. Thinking of going into the lucrative field of archaeological consulting? First, read this short novel, or another in the series: *Burial Ground: An Alan Graham Mystery*, by Malcolm Shuman (New York: Avon, 1998). The author gives a very realistic depiction of the life of a contract archaeologist (except for all the murders, that is), and it's a good read, too. For another kind of fantasy, the Sandia Cave controversy is presented in journalistic style in D. Preston's article, "The Mystery of Sandia Cave," *The New Yorker*, 12 June 1995, 66–83. In case you're wondering if archaeologists really do have ethics, read about them in *Archaeological Ethics*, edited by Karen Vitelli and Chip Colwell-Chanthaphonh (Lanham, Md.: AltaMira Press, 2006). For an enjoyable tour of forgeries, naive misinterpretations, and pseudoscience, I recommend *Frauds, Myths, and Mysteries: Science and Pseudoscience in Archaeology*, by Kenneth Feder (New York: Mayfield Press, 2001).

Chapter 3. The New Archeology and Its Predecessors

The best survey of archaeological ideas is *A History of Archaeological Thought*, by Bruce Trigger (Cambridge: Cambridge University Press,

1989). For an original and controversial view of history and archaeology from the 1930s, see if you can find a copy of *Man Makes Himself*, by V. Gordon Childe (London: Watts, 1936). Those who just can't get enough of the New Archeology might try *A Study in Archaeology*, by Walter Taylor (Memoir 69, American Anthropological Association, 1948). The statement that may have ushered in the New Archeology is "Archaeology as Anthropology," by Lewis Binford, *American Antiquity* 28 (1962): 217–25. It's also a premier example of the kind of jargon-riddled writing that still plagues our field. For a stunning view of what some New Archeologists achieved, take a stroll through *The Early Mesoamerican Village*, edited by Kent Flannery (New York: Academic Press, 1976).

Chapter 4. Ethnoarchaeology and Cultural Ecology

The story of Lew and Eskimos can be read in greater detail in Lewis Binford's *Nunamiut Ethnoarchaeology* (New York: Academic Press, 1982). A very different approach to ethnoarchaeology is taken in *Symbols in Action*, by Ian Hodder (Cambridge: Cambridge University Press, 1982). To see how a British archaeologist began to tease out the complex relationship between culture and environment, try *Excavations at Starr Carr*, by Grahame Clark (Cambridge: Cambridge University Press, 1954). A version of this classic case study is frequently reprinted as an educational module by Addison-Wesley.

Chapter 5. Diffusion and Classifying Societies

My discussion of bands, chiefdoms, and the rest comes from *Primitive Social Organization*, by Elman Service (New York: Random House, 1971). Although the author presents his scheme as social *evolution*, I prefer to think of it as a purely descriptive model. Diffusion of ideas is a fact (there, I said the word), but in itself it doesn't really explain much—as the New Archeologists insisted—and it can be deceptive. An example of the extreme (and extremely unscholarly) use of diffusion as explanation is *Bronze Age America*, by Barry Fell (Boston: Little, Brown, 1982). It's a good laugh, but I don't take it seriously.

Chapter 6. Cannibalism and the Native Peoples/Archaeology Relationship

Was cannibalism largely the invention of nineteenth-century Europeans who wanted to rationalize their imperialist tendencies? This position is taken by W. Arens in *The Man-Eating Myth* (New York: Oxford University Press, 1979). A very different view of the controversy comes from that other institution (Cambridge) in *Divine Hunger*, by Peggy Sanday (Cambridge: Cambridge University Press, 1986). If you read only one book on cannibalism this year, make it the latter. Archaeology's love/hate relationship with Native Americans is exposed in *Skull Wars: Archaeology and the Search for Native American Identity*, by David Hurst Thomas (New York: Basic Books, 2000). Thomas, an internationally respected scholar with an excellent writing style, puts the Kennewick Man controversy in historical context.

Chapter 7. Gender

For a review of how archaeologists worldwide are tackling the issue, try *In Pursuit of Gender*, by Sarah Nelson and Myriam Rosen-Ayalan (Walnut Creek, Calif.: AltaMira Press, 2002), or Nelson's edited volume (also from AltaMira) *Handbook of Gender in Archaeology* (2006). My discussion of Aztec women's work comes from Elizabeth Brumfiel's "Weaving and Cooking," in *Engendering Archaeology*, edited by Joan Gero and Margaret Conkey (Oxford: Blackwell, 1991), 224–51. To learn how women's roles changed among the Inca, I recommend "Gender, Space, and Food in Prehistory," by Christina Hastorf, in *Engendering Archaeology*, 132–59. Those fascinated by the concept of a third gender and the method of ethnohistory should read Sandra Holliman's "The Third Gender in Native California," in *Women in Prehistory*, edited by Cheryl Claassen and Rosemary Joyce (Philadelphia: University of Pennsylvania Press, 1997), 173–88. *Are All Warriors Male?* ask archaeologists Katheryn Linduff and Karen Rubinson (Lanham, Md.: AltaMira Press, 2008). Turns out that that they weren't.

Chapter 8. Marxist-Influenced Archaeology

To learn more about how the chieftains of Neolithic Sweden may have used material culture to maintain their power, try this rather complex chapter by Christopher Tilley: "Ideology and the Legitimating of Power in the Middle Neolithic of Southern Sweden," in *Ideology, Power, and Prehistory*, edited by Daniel Miller and Christopher Tilley (Cambridge: Cambridge University Press, 1984), 111–46. If you're interested in seeing where other archaeologists have taken the ideas of Uncle Karl, I recommend *The Archaeology of Inequality*, edited by Randall McGuire and Robert Paynter (Oxford: Blackwell, 1991). The editors' introductory essay is particularly good. Learn about the lives of miners and the 1914 Ludlow Massacre from a group of Marxist-influenced archaeologists who investigated the Colorado Coal Field War and published their "Archaeology of the Colorado Coal Field War" as the Ludlow Collective (in *Archaeologies of the Contemporary Past*, edited by V. Buchli and Gavin Lucas; London: Routledge, 2001, 94–107).

Chapter 9. Agency and Neoevolutionism

I can't recommend actually reading Anthony Giddens's writing on structuration. Frankly, it's pretty heavy going. But Pierre Bourdieu's work is easier for an anthropologist like me to follow, as it is more ethnography than sociology—see, for example, *The Logic of Practice* (Cambridge: Polity Press, 1990). To see how an archaeologist uses the idea, try Arthur Joyce's short article on "The Founding of Monte Alban," in *Agency in Archaeology*, edited by Marcia-Anne Dobres and John Robb (London: Routledge, 2000), 71–91. I've used a lot of Pat Kirch's work in this chapter and can recommend his article "The Evolution of Sociopolitical Complexity in Prehistoric Hawai'i," *Journal of World Prehistory* 4 (1990): 311–45.

Chapter 10. Postprocessual Archaeologies

The postprocessual box holds more ideas than I can unpack here. Michael Shanks (or at least I think it was he) called it "archaeology with attitude." Here are a couple of books that give a feel for the subject, though I'm not sure that my first author would approve of being put in this category. But somewhere I have to mention a very influential book that is cited by scholars and is fun to read (inexpensive, too): *In Small Things Forgotten: An Archaeology of Early American Life*, by James Deetz (New York: Anchor Books, 1996). A thoroughly postprocessual, "reflexive" approach to archaeology is offered in *The Archaeological Process*, by Ian Hodder (Oxford: Blackwell, 1999). Hodder's final chapter, "Towards Nondichotomous Thinking in Archaeology," presents a radical new approach that redefines archaeological evidence and challenges old notions about who has the right to interpret it. Excellent stuff.

INDEX

ABOUT THE AUTHOR/ILLUSTRATOR

Adrian Praetzellis' first archaeological fieldwork was on the famous site at Mucking, in southern England. Here he spent July of 1969 schlepping wheelbarrows full of gravel in the rain. Eschewing the trades of bricklayer's laborer and assembly-line worker, Adrian devoted the early 1970s to learning the field archaeologist's craft by digging Roman and medieval sites on the British archaeological "circuit." Tired of living in tents and derelict buildings, in 1975 he and his wife, Mary, decided to seek their fortune in California. Since the late 1970s, Adrian has specialized in urban historical archaeology, focusing on ethnicity, cultural change, and social boundary maintenance as viewed through the archaeology and history of the Overseas Chinese, Jews, and other immigrant groups in the American West.

In spite of not finishing high school (it's a long story), Adrian has a PhD in anthropology from the University of California, Berkeley. Since 1992, he has taught archaeology and cultural resources management at Sonoma State University, where he is professor of anthropology and director of the Anthropological Studies Center, a university research institute. Adrian is also the author/illustrator of *Dug to Death: A Tale of Archaeological Method and Mayhem* (2003).